JANI KAY

Jani is a voracious reader and would spend her last dime on a book. She's always found it fascinating that, merely for the price of a book, she can escape her world for a while and explore an entirely different one through someone else's eyes.

Besides reading, her favorite pastime is traveling. She has traveled the world, learning about other cultures and customs, and realizing that, no matter where we live, we all ultimately want the same things.

Ever since she can remember, Jani wanted to write stories about people, and about their lives and loves. Exciting relationships and shared happiness are at the core of her novels; these are arguably the most difficult achievements to master in life, and yet this is what we all desire.

Jani used to scrapbook until the small hours of the night, but these days she keeps the midnight oil burning by chatting online with her loyal readers. To Jani, writing is her passion, and communicating with her readers is her joy.

Jani lives in Perth, Western Australia, with her husband. They have two children.

*****

Jani would love to hear from you.
Please email her at:
janikaybooks@gmail.com

Copyright

Editing:
Ryder — Prequel: Gina Kempton
Two Worlds Colliding: Lauren McKellar

Cover Design:
© Arijana Karčić, Cover It! Designs

Formatting:
Angels Indie Formatting
angelsindieformatting@yahoo.com.au

ISBN: 978-0-9923090-6-0

By the Same Author

Standalone Novel
Open Your Eyes

Firebird Series
Lost in France (Book 1)

No Regrets (Book 2)

Scorpio Stinger MC Series
Ryder — Prequel (Book 0.5)

The Beginning: A Duet (Ryder Prequel &
Two Worlds Colliding in a single volume)

Unchain My Heart (Book 2)

A Biker Christmas Novella (Book 2.5)

Gods & Monsters (Book 3)

Love on Wall Street Series
Debonair (Part 1)

Dedication

This book is for my son, a real Scorpio.
I LOVE YOU.
Unconditionally. Forever.
Be the best you can be.

To ALL my loved ones — family and friends,
who deeply touch my heart and my soul.
I love you. More than you will ever know.
Thank you for your support and believing in me.
It means the world to me.

*****

Thank You

Thank you for purchasing and reading my books.
I hope you enjoy this story.

NOTE FROM THE AUTHOR

Ryder has a foul mouth and a dirty mind and doesn't think much of women after being deserted by his mother as a kid — he's a MC biker — one who had a ROUGH childhood . . . and it reflects in the way he talks and thinks and speaks to and about women.

Expect BAD things in his past . . . it's what makes him the person he is . . .

As an author, Jani Kay respects your right to know before purchasing the Scorpion Stinger MC Series and to make a decision based on that information. She also reserves the right to portray her characters as she sees them, warts and all.

Ryder is what he is — no apologies.

*****

This book is intended for mature audiences (18+) who are not offended or squeamish about extreme language or graphic sexual situations.

It is purely FICTION.

THE PRINCESS & THE BIKER

A modern day Romeo and Juliet romance

Ryder Knox wants freedom from the hatred churning in his gut. Saved by the **Scorpio Stingers MC** boys, he owes his life and allegiance to them—they are his family. He doesn't need a smart mouthed woman who pushes every one of his buttons. But he can't get Jade out of his head.

Jade Summers is a good girl. She wants a man just like her lawyer daddy. Not the alpha male biker who storms into her life, who looks like a sex god with tattoos and piercings. He's demanding, controlling and won't take no for an answer. Their chemistry is off the charts and they are drawn to one another like magnets. Neither can resist the other.

Two worlds collide. Their families are determined to tear them apart. With everything stacked against them, is what they have strong enough to overcome the odds? They must choose: family or one another. The ultimate price may be too high. Will their polar opposite worlds destroy and rip them apart forever?

SCORPIO STINGER MC

Two Worlds Colliding

Adult Contemporary Romance Novel

USA TODAY & INTERNATIONAL
Bestselling Author

JANI KAY

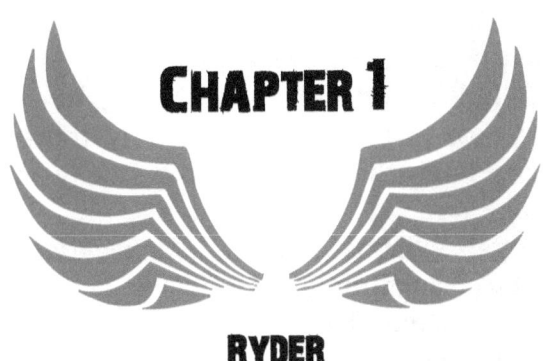

CHAPTER 1

RYDER

"Princess," I groaned, "you're killing me here."

My head hurt. Why in fuck's name did I let this woman get under my skin? I knew she'd be trouble, from the first day I walked into the agency.

But no, my cock knew better. It just had to get the fuck inside that pussy of hers.

Yeah.

And now I was screwed in so many ways, it felt like a punch to my gut.

Jade was a stubborn woman—she wasn't going to make this easy. But fuck that. Her pussy was mine now, and nobody was gonna stop me from getting more.

Not even her, or her family.

She doesn't know what a persistent fuck I am.

Tenacious. Determined.

I take what I want. And at this moment, it was the girl I'd just fucked on my bike.

And THAT was a big deal. 'Cause I'd never fucked any bitch on the back of my bike. Was never going to either.

Until Jade.

I'd never wanted anyone this much. She fucked with my mind. I thought of her all the time—day and night. And now that I'd tasted her pussy, there was no going back. I knew that as sure as I knew my name was Ryder Knox.

Ryder gets what Ryder wants. *Not negotiable.*

Her voice caught in her throat. "It's because you're not listening to me, Ryder. I said from the start that we'd have this one night only. Don't you get that?"

Her eyes glistened in the dark. Was she fucking tearing up? Uneasy, I rubbed her back, soothing her.

"I did . . . I do. But now . . . I want *more . . .* of you." I groaned.

Yeah, I was cunt-struck and I knew it. I'd thought once I'd had her, I'd be able to get rid of my obsession with her and her pussy. Turns out it only made me want her more. And she was resisting me. *Fuck.*

"It's impossible, Ryder. You've got to believe me." She wasn't bitchy, or sarcastic, or anything like she usually was. This worried me even more. It meant she was serious as all hell.

"Babe, I'm going to get you home now. You're tired, and you're cold. But we're gonna talk. Real soon. And I ain't taking no for an answer."

Jade nodded, trembling in my arms. I gripped her ass and pulled her to me, pushing my hardness against her stomach. One more kiss. I had to have just one more . . . I lifted her face to mine and kissed the shit out of her. She had to know how much I wanted her.

She sighed into my mouth, and melted her soft curves into my hardness. I took her mouth again, sucking at her lips. I figured a man was entitled to some happiness—however fleeting. But there was no way in hell I was getting attached to Jade. Oh no, I'd let my cock have its way with her; I'd fuck her as much as I needed. But that was all.

Being a realist, I knew it couldn't last forever because nothing ever did, as if the fucking universe hated me. As soon as I loved somebody as my own, they left me. First Marianne, and then Max. I understood about Max, so I was OK with that. Didn't hurt any less, though. His moving to New York, on the other side of the fucking country, was as good as if he'd moved to a different planet.

Reluctantly, I pulled away. Had to get back to the house. Shaking my head to clear the sex-fog in my brain, I got onto the bike.

"Get on," I growled.

Fuck. Looking at her standing there, her arms wrapped around herself, biting her lip, I just wanted to take her to my bed. And then bury myself deep inside her. *All night long.*

She hitched her dress up her thighs, exposing the milky-white skin above her stockings where the lacy tops ended. My cock twitched. I couldn't tear my eyes away. Fuck, I wanted her again.

Her arms came around me as she scooted as close as she could get to me on the bike. Princess was asking for it. I was taking her home. Yeah. That's what I was going to do.

"Hold on, babe." My chest tightened. Jesus, she affected me in ways I didn't know a woman could.

The bike roared to life, rumbling under my ass. I took a deep calming breath, then another, deep into my stomach. This feeling I understood—my bike and I had a great relationship. Bitches and I, not so much.

CHAPTER 2

JADE

Slipping my arms around Ryder, I thrust my body against his, needing to be as close to him as humanly possible. I wanted to soak him in, to feel his warmth, and to smell him. Experience every inch of him and burn this into my memory so that later, I could unpack it all and savor tonight over and over for as long as I needed to.

I squeezed my eyes shut—I wasn't getting through to Ryder. He wouldn't listen to what I was trying so hard to make him understand: we were from two different worlds.

Mutually exclusive worlds.

My world wouldn't accept him as much as his wouldn't accept me.

Anything between us had to end tonight. There was no other way, especially if there was to be no bloodshed. What we had was a strong physical attraction—

nothing else. My stomach churned, and bile rose in my throat.

This could be one of the best or one of the worst nights of my life.

Harrison would go ballistic if he just *saw* Ryder. He'd shoot first, and ask questions later. Since that day almost ten years ago, his hatred of bikers and their kind had turned him into a coldhearted man. In fact, he'd get pleasure out of watching Ryder die a slow and tortured death. For Amy. And the others, too, but *mostly* for Amy.

I sighed deeply, drawing the smell of him into my nostrils on an inhale. I'd let him get me close to home and then I'd catch a taxi back to the house.

It was time I found my own place. Living with my parents had worked for me, up until tonight. Now I needed my own space. I didn't want to answer to them anymore. It'd never bothered me before, but now I was an adult and it was time to take full responsibility for myself. My twenty-third birthday was only weeks away—it was time to move out.

Ryder made the trip back toward the city a lot faster than when we'd come up Mulholland Drive earlier. I had to hold on with all my might, our bodies moving as one as he rounded sharp bends, leaning together as the beast roared beneath us.

The cool wind whipped my hair all over my face. It was useless trying to tame it, so I just went with the flow and closed my eyes, feeling the ride rather than watching. Every bump, every acceleration was amplified with my eyes closed.

Eventually I heard other traffic noises, so I knew we were approaching built-up areas. Ryder slowed and stopped at what I assumed was a traffic light. I ventured my eyes open and gasped. We were in the driveway of the house in Beverly Hills already.

A smile crossed my lips. Ryder had listened to me after all. He was going to call a taxi to take me home.

"Off, babe," he ordered, his voice a deep growl.

I jumped off the bike and tried to straighten my windswept hair. I was sure I looked a hot mess with my clingy dress still up around the top of my thighs—the dress I had chosen, because tonight was the night I was going to give in to Marcus and have sex with him.

Before that plan turned to shit.

A wry smile crossed my lips. The evening turned out nothing like I'd expected. I'd ended up fucking a man so completely different to Marcus in every imaginable way, yet it was exactly what I'd needed.

Ryder's long leg swung over the bike and he stood in front of me, a naughty grin on his face.

"Was that good for you too?" he drawled, his eyes hooded so that I couldn't see if he was being sarcastic or just teasing me.

"It was fun. Thanks. But now I need to call a taxi to get me home. My parents will be worried about where I am."

"No. No cab. You're staying here tonight. With me."

Is he serious?

Stunned, I shook my head. "I can't, I need to go..."

He took a step closer and pressed a thumb against my lips. *Hard.* "Shut up, woman. You talk too much. Always fighting me."

He lifted my chin and his mouth possessed mine, my resistance fading as I melted into him. My arms curled around his neck and twisted his hair as his lips possessed mine. Sense left my brain, and my core clenched. His large hand squeezed my ass, pressing me to him. I was wet already.

How was it possible that he had this effect on me? It was as if I were in a trance around him. Shaking my head, I pushed against his chest.

Get going now, Jade, before you can't walk away.

"Ryder, I've *got* to go—"

"*Got* to do plenty, Princess. But I know you don't *want* to. There's a difference."

"I'm calling a taxi." I reached into my purse for my phone and started dialing.

He yanked it right out of my hand. I gasped and lunged at him, trying to grab it, but he was too tall, holding it above his head. His eyes narrowed and he stared down at me, a satisfied sneer on his face.

"Ryder, please." I huffed, arms folded across my chest, pouting. I wasn't in the mood for games. I'd had enough shit for one night.

"You *will* be begging me tonight. *But not to leave.*"

My eyebrow quirked. "I'm going home, like it or not."

He continued as if I hadn't said a word. "You'll be begging me to make you come. Yeah." He smirked.

"No. It's over, and I'm lea—"

Big strong arms lifted me off my feet as if I were a feather. Next thing, I was hanging ass-up over Ryder's shoulder.

"Dammit, Ryder. Put me down." I squealed.

"Hush, you'll wake Mia and the kids." He strode toward the house with long determined steps.

I was equally single-minded. My fists pounded his back. "Put me down!"

I jerked as a hard slap landed on my ass.

"Quiet," he growled.

"No!" I shouted.

Another smack. Harder. My ass stung like hell.

"Jade," he hissed. Even though I couldn't see his face, I knew he was clenching his jaw in that *Ryder* way he did so well. He set me down at the front door, his arm an iron cage around my waist, his hand covering my mouth. My eyes widened when I looked up into his. They were dark and stormy.

"Now listen the fuck up. You're staying. You can fight, but you can't run." He removed his hand from my mouth warily. "I'm going to unlock the door now. Think of Mia and the kids, and for fuck's sake keep quiet. We don't want to wake them at two in the morning. OK?"

I nodded. I didn't want Mia to see me like this. And I didn't want to disturb the little ones' sleep. I'd wait till we got to his room before I attempted my escape. He had to let me go—nothing good could come from this.

Without a word, he knelt down in front of me, his hands on the backs of my thighs, ensuring I wasn't going anywhere. Sweet Jesus, what was he going to do to me now? My heart beat erratically in my chest, my pussy clenching as his warm breath caressed over my skin.

His face was right in front of my sex. He took a deep breath.

Jesus. *Shit.*

My panties flooded with my juices. I couldn't stop them even if I wanted to.

"Ahhh, fuck," Ryder groaned, his voice primal and guttural.

I sucked in a breath, my knees growing weak. He lifted a foot onto his knee.

What the hell?

I closed my eyes.

Oh sweet Jesus, I wanted his mouth on me.

I expected him to dive in under my dress that was hardly covering my mound. Instead he let out a deep sigh and removed my shoe. He set my foot down again, and proceeded to do the same with the other foot.

I stood barefoot in front of him now, his face inches from my pussy.

He chuckled softly and licked the exposed skin on top of my thigh, just above where the lace of my stocking ended. By now, my legs were trembling. He gripped my hips and jerked me toward his face, then pushed my legs open and my thong to the side, nose-diving straight into my wetness. His tongue tasted me in one long swoop.

"Christ," he groaned, "so fucking wet for me."

He plunged two fingers inside. I whimpered, opening my legs wider, like a slut wanting more. My fingers tangled in his hair, holding his head to my sex. I was practically fucking his face—in front of the open door.

Ryder stood up quickly, my shoes clattering to the ground as he lifted me into his arms.

"Got to have you now," he hissed. "You're so ready for fucking."

I leaned my head against his chest and breathed him in. *He smelled like sex.* God, what was it about this man that messed with my head so much I couldn't think straight?

"Hmmm," I moaned, unable to produce a coherent sentence.

He carried me in through the dimly lit hallway to the guest room where I had fallen asleep with the kids a few weeks ago. I hadn't known then that this was where Ryder slept. I'd assumed Mia was his woman, and that he slept with her in the master bedroom. A twinge stabbing at my heart made me realize how little I liked the idea of Ryder fucking Mia.

No, I wanted Ryder to fuck me. *And only me.*

He pushed the door closed with the back of his foot and set me down on the bed. My eyes were still adjusting to the darkness of the room when I heard a belt buckle crashing to the floor, and then the slide of a zipper. He clapped his hands twice, and the bedside lamps lit up automatically.

I gasped. His beautiful erection was standing proud, thick veins from his cock pulsing, pre-cum on the tip glowing in the soft light.

I licked my lips involuntarily.

Ryder grinned, knowing exactly what I wanted. *To taste him.*

He crawled up the bed, covering my body with his. He pushed my dress up to my waist.

Sucking in a breath, he warned me. "This is going to be hard and fast, Princess. We have the rest of the night to fuck slowly. There will be no sleeping."

I swallowed hard.

"You can taste me. Later. Now I'm going to fuck the shit out of your pussy that's already so wet for me."

He sat back and pushed my legs open, his thick fingers wrapping around the thin elastic of my thong, and with a strong jerk, he ripped them right off my body.

I was fully exposed to his eyes for the first time.

"Fuck, you're *beautiful*," he growled, his eyes on fire.

Coming from Ryder, that was the best compliment I'd ever had.

His thumb circled my clit, pushing my need for him up another notch. I whimpered, needy, ready, wanting him inside me.

Ryder didn't disappoint. He took his cock in his hand and rubbed the pre-cum over the tip with his thumb. I drew in a breath—watching him being so primal was erotic beyond words. He quickly rolled a condom on and nudged my opening, rubbing his cock in my wet folds, lubricating himself so he would slide into me like a hot knife into butter.

Jesus, it was sexy. My pussy was throbbing—my heartbeat in my sex. Frantic. Wild. Ready.

He thrust into me with a feral animalistic groan, his hips bucking as he fucked me hard. No slow stroking, no stretching me first. He was as caveman as a guy could get.

And I loved it.

He bit into my shoulder, his balls slapping against my ass as he drove into me again and again.

I slipped my arms under his T-shirt and dug my nails into his skin, pushing my heels into his ass so he would go deeper.

"Greedy little cunt," Ryder rasped.

"Yes," I hissed. I knew it, and right now I didn't care, as long as he kept fucking me hard. I'd never been fucked like this before, and I knew that after this, I could never go back to gentle-only again.

"Going to come, babe. Your pussy's so tight."

Damn, his dirty mouth turned me on, his words pushing me over the edge.

"Me . . . me too," I moaned, trying my best to be quiet. I definitely didn't want Mia or the kids waking and hearing our sexual grunting noises.

"Come." His voice was husky yet demanding.

Just that one word and I spiraled out of control, my sex clenching wildly, gripping his cock as I rode my orgasm, thrusting my hips to meet his.

"Fuck, bitch . . . Princess . . . Jade. Fuck."

He let go, pumping into me violently as he bit into my neck.

Our chests heaved, our breathing out of control, desperate for air, our bodies trembling as we held one another.

"Never." Ryder panted. "Never . . . had a woman like you. You're *my bitch,* now. Only mine. That pussy is

11

mine."

I laughed softly. Yeah, I was his bitch. And my pussy was definitely his.

For now, at least.

Tomorrow? Hell, I didn't know.

CHAPTER 3

RYDER

Princess had me by the balls. Every time I got inside her pussy, it just made me crave more. I couldn't get enough of her.

I knew without a doubt that I couldn't settle for anything less. There was something so different with Jade, a tugging at my heart and soul I'd never felt before. I was in fucking unknown territory. Usually it excited the hell out of me—I thrived on challenges and exploring new opportunities. But this was on another level completely.

I wasn't sure I wanted to understand what was going on with me.

"Ryder, I've got to go," she whispered, her face buried in my neck.

"No." I grunted. "Stay."

"My family—"

I couldn't let her go. "I'm not done with you, babe.

That was just the start."

"Yeah? And then, Ryder? What about tomorrow, and the next day? It just gets harder the more we do this."

I looked into her eyes. They were sad.

"Night ain't over, Princess. You said we had one night. Till the sun rises you're still mine."

"Ryder," she gasped.

"Call your family. That's what phones are for. Tell them you're safe, and that you aren't coming home tonight."

She stared at me for a long time. Different emotions flickered through her eyes. I watched in amazement as she battled with her inner self. Would she stay? Did she understand how much I wanted her?

After what felt like forever, the ends of her mouth curved up ever-so-slightly.

I'd won.

"OK. But only tonight. When the sun rises, *it's over.* Deal?"

I grinned. It wasn't exactly the answer I'd wanted, but it would do. For now. Tomorrow I'd make other plans.

"Deal." I nodded my head.

She sat up, and opened her purse to find her phone. She quickly dialed the number and spoke to her father. From their conversation I gathered that her old man was relieved that she was OK, but he wasn't happy that she wasn't coming home. Jade evaded his questions about where she was, and what had happened, telling him that they'd discuss it when she was back.

She's going to be a kick-ass lawyer.

I grabbed two beers from the mini-bar fridge in my room. Yeah, go figure. This guest room was more like a hotel suite. It had a large desk as well as a seating area

14

with two couches. The bathroom was five-star—not that I'd really know as I'd never seen anything as fancy as that. It featured an enormous bath—big enough for an orgy—and had massaging jets and gold taps. *The shit rich people spent their cash on . . .*

Jade must've been thirsty 'cause she leaned against the headboard and gulped the beer down. Or was she using the alcohol to calm her nerves?

My gaze raked her body. I wanted to see what was under her dress. I wanted my hands on her perky tits. With Mia and the kids in the house, I couldn't do to her what I really wanted to, but I knew we'd get to that in time.

My dick was still half-mast, ready for more action, but slower this time. At least, I'd try to go slower. When my need for her overtook me, I became wild and frantic, almost ape-like in my desire for her.

No wonder she called me a caveman . . .

"Tell me about your brother?" The bed dipped as I sat my naked ass beside her.

"What do you want to know?" she asked, casting her eyes down. Yeah, she was going to pull the lawyer trick on me, too. She was going to evade my questions.

"You said he was a mean-ass cop." I took a long sip of my beer. Damn it tasted good. "Tell me more?"

"Oh, he's with Special Ops. I don't know all that much. Harrison's pretty secretive about it. All I know it has to do with protecting our country against terrorists and eliminating illegal weapons. He won't tell me more. For my own protection, he said." Her eyes were cast down, and there was a sadness tugging at the corners of her mouth as she spoke about him.

She sighed heavily. Suspecting there was more to the story, I kept silent, encouraging her to keep talking. She fell silent for a while, and just as I was about to give up on her offering more information, she spoke again.

"Ten years ago, something terrible happened that changed him forever. And me, too." She closed her eyes as if to hide her pain.

My head jerked up. Now I fucking had to know more. I narrowed my eyes and watched her, still staying silent even though I had a hundred questions running through my brain.

"What happened?" I asked softly when she went all quiet. She was so deep in her thoughts I worried she'd fallen asleep.

"It was all my fault. What happened to Amy. And the others." She bit her lower lip, her chin quivering. Fuck, she was going to cry. I hated when women cried. I never knew what the fuck to do.

"Princess, it's OK." Pulling her foot onto my lap, I stroked it, massaging her soles with my thumb. Her shoulders relaxed slightly and she blew out a long heavy breath.

"I haven't spoken about it in years. More than seven, actually. After my therapy, I locked it away in a file in my brain and I tried to forget it ever happened. I'm trying to just move on with my life. *Without* the guilt."

What in fuck's name could have happened? And who was Amy? And what did it have to do with Harrison? So many fucking questions, but I didn't want to harass her with my curiosity. At least, not yet.

Clearly it was a big deal. Tears were streaming down Jade's cheeks. Fuck, I hadn't meant to bring her pain. I knew all about burying the hurt so deep that it got lost in a dark corner of one's soul.

"Babe. It's OK." I put both our empty beer bottles on the table, and scooted over to hold her. Seeing my woman less than happy had a strange effect on me, twisting my heart and squeezing the fuck out of it.

Jade rubbed at her chest, then looked up at me with her big blue eyes. Fuck, I drowned in those eyes. For a minute there the world stood still.

Then she started laughing. Yeah. *Laughing.*

"Babe. You OK?" Was she losing the plot?

"You look so funny wearing only a tee and socks."

She was right. It wasn't my best look. I'd never cared what a bitch thought before. Why did I suddenly care now? I leaned over and pulled off my socks, throwing them into the corner.

"Better?" I grinned.

She quirked an eyebrow. "The tee?"

I pulled it over my head, and sent it to join my socks.

This woman was going to be the best fucking lawyer in the state.

She had question-evasion down to an art.

CHAPTER 4

JADE

Stunned, I sucked in a breath.

I'd changed the subject purposely to distract Ryder from asking too many questions. But I'd never bargained on getting totally distracted myself.

Ryder was magnificent. His body was lean, yet muscled, with large pecs and washboard abs that left me speechless. The hardness of his body was such a strong contrast to my own soft curves that it had me salivating just at the thought of running my fingers over his skin to feel that hardness beneath my palms.

My gaze followed the deep V that flanked his groin and came to rest on his cock. A smile twitched the corners of my mouth as I admired both the length and breadth of the beast that had ravaged me and driven me to orgasm.

Yes, Ryder Knox was a fine specimen of alpha-maleness indeed. And tonight he was mine. All mine.

His sculpted body and artful tattoos took my breath away. If I'd ever been on the fence before about an inked body, I was a convert now. I traced a finger up his arm, following the tattoo of the cobra's tail from the top of Ryder's hand, curling its way up his forearm to his bicep and triceps. His muscles flexed in reaction to my feather-like strokes. Curling my fingers, I squeezed his upper arm. Feeling his brute strength flipped my stomach and made my pussy clench. Here was a man who could protect me against harm. It was intoxicating.

My hand floated over his chest toward the tattoo above his heart. It was beautiful; a red and yellow exotic bird with a long sweeping tail that ended just above his nipple. I sucked in a breath when my eyes fell on his nipple ring. God, it was sexy. I had to touch it. I dipped my head and licked his nipple, sucking gently on the piercing.

The feral groan that rumbled from his chest made my heart sing. I liked that I could affect him this much.

My tongue traced down the center of his torso, kissing and lapping its way south, passed the sprinkling of hair that took me directly to the pot of gold. I ignored his cock, which by now had grown in length and width, and was bobbing its head for my attention. I kissed the V on each side of his loin, eliciting an even deeper groan.

"Fuck, babe. What are you doing to me?" I looked up at him from under my lashes. His pupils were fully dilated, a fine mist of sweat covering his skin.

I went in for the kill. Without touching him with my hands, I licked the pre-cum from his tip before rimming his cock with my mouth. Listening for his panting breaths, I gauged how well I was doing, increasing the pressure of my lips as I ran them up and down his shaft.

"Suck me," he demanded, grabbing a fist full of hair and pushing his cock into my mouth. I took him deep, nearly balls-deep. He was too big to take all the way without gagging, so I quickly fisted the base of his cock to fully envelop him.

I sucked.

He groaned.

I pumped his cock with my fist till he pulled my head right back, releasing his cock.

"Jesus. You'll make me come if you keep that up for another second."

I licked my lips and smiled up at him. The expression on his face was priceless: half-dazed, half in agony, I knew he was close to the point of no return.

Ryder pulled me up his body, and I felt my hardened nipples scrape along his skin. He let out a long hiss. Holding the back of my head, he kissed me long and hard, every ounce of his longing poured into that one kiss. Finally he released my mouth.

"Ride me. Make me come hard," he ordered, his voice gruff.

Yes.

I was dying to get his cock inside me. I ripped the foil with my teeth, barely caring if I bit a hole in the fucking condom, I was that desperate to have him fill me. My fingers trembled as I placed it onto the tip of his cock. He sensed my uncertainty and covered my hands with his, helping me to roll it on. Shit, it was sexy as hell. I squeezed my thighs together, the ache in my pussy becoming unbearable.

"Eager, Princess?" he murmured, chuckling softly.

I nodded. We were equally desperate, and this wasn't the time for talking.

Pushing upward, I lifted my body and his hands cupped my ass and squeezed. "Perfect. Your ass is perfect."

I smiled back at him as I took his cock in my hand

and guided it to my waiting entrance.

"Ryder," I gasped as his hands guided me down and his cock drove into me, filling me to the hilt.

"Good girl." It was a fullness I loved experiencing.

"Now ride me," he said, a smile twisting the corners of his mouth as he reached up and grabbed my breasts in both hands and squeezed hard.

Finding strength in my thighs, I rode his cock, slamming down onto his balls each time. He pulled me forward and sucked a nipple into his mouth before biting down on the hard nub. I squealed, trying hard not to make a noise. The combination of pleasure and pain drove me to the edge.

His fingers found their way to my clit and he circled the sensitive bud till all my senses exploded. "Ryder. Please. I'm going to come." I panted, frantic for release.

"Come, baby. Come for me." His voice was husky, and his command sent me over the edge.

I let go. "Yes. *Baby*," I breathed, my voice barely above a whisper. Wave after wave of delicious ripples passed through my body, gripping his cock as I convulsed around him.

"Fuck. That's it for me too."

His eyes rolled back in his head before he closed them and I watched his beautiful face as he came apart, pumping into me.

He pulled me to his chest and I lay on top of him. His arms tightened around me, his chest heaving with exertion. He planted a kiss on my forehead.

Completely sated, we fell asleep as the birds started twittering outside, a sure sign that dawn was approaching.

CHAPTER 5

JADE

The morning had come all too quickly, and Ryder and I had dozed off in one another's arms, exhausted, sweaty, and thoroughly fucked. I would probably still be sleeping if it weren't for my phone waking me. I let it go to voicemail.

Since I was awake, I decided to get home before Ryder woke and tried to stop me. I slipped on my dress and tiptoed to the door. Luckily Ryder was out cold, so I snuck out of the house and found my shoes by the front door. I walked to the sidewalk before I called for a taxi.

While I waited for the taxi, I scrolled through the nine text messages Marcus had left me. Then I listened to the thirteen voice messages, deleting them one by one. From what I could gather, Marcus was in a spin; he'd left the party and gone home, avoiding my father so that he didn't need to explain to him that I'd caught him with his pants down and his dick inside the new secretary. Or that I'd gone off on the back of a badass biker's motorcycle. I suppressed the urge to giggle, thinking of Marcus and his panicked expression when we rode off, leaving him on the sidewalk.

I didn't think Marcus ever imagined that *good girl* Jade would really go through with something like that. And he was right—a mere few months ago I wouldn't have dreamed that I'd behave like this. Jesus, I would've slapped a libel suit on anyone who dared to degrade and insult me with such an accusation.

Now, here I was, sneaking to my bedroom like a teenager, my shoes in my hand, wearing Ryder's shirt over my dress. I looked a goddamn mess, and I hoped I could get to my room before being spotted and interrogated.

"Jade, is that you, honey?" Mom's voice was laced with worry.

"Yes, I'm home. And everything's fine."

She caught me just as I reached my bedroom. Her eyes narrowed and she drew a deep breath. "I'm glad you're safe. But you had me really worried. It's not like you, Jade. You didn't even behave like this when you were younger..."

"I know. And maybe I should've. Because I grew up to quickly, and never had a chance to just be a crazy teenager."

"Then why start now? Who is the man that you slept with last night? I know it's not Marcus. And good Lord, you look a mess. Must've been a rough night."

Mom never sugarcoated her words. I appreciated that about her, because I always knew exactly where I stood.

"Daddy?" I enquired, yawning behind my hand. My eyes were about to fall closed. I'd hardly slept and after the vigorous . . . *exercise* Ryder had put me through, I was sore and tired.

She shook her head. "He's asleep. I gave him something to help him doze off. Go have a shower, Jade. I'll bring you a cup of tea. Looks like you could do with it."

I shot her a grateful glance. I wasn't off the hook—I knew Sylvia Summers better than that—but she'd let me clean up and sleep first, so that I was up to the full-on interrogation that lay ahead.

"Dad called Harrison. Just thought you should know. All Marcus said after Dad finally got through to his phone is that you left on the back of a *motorcycle*. Is that true?" A small smile twisted the corners of her mouth. She was the one who'd taught me to always know the rules so that I could break them properly if need be.

I nodded. "Yes. But there's much more to the story that I'm sure Marcus didn't bother to elaborate on."

She gave me a knowing smile. "As there always is. I'll go make that tea now, and we can talk later."

As soon as she left, I went for a shower. The sooner I washed the smell of Ryder off my body, the better. He'd covered every inch of my skin with his mouth, and as I touched myself while soaping up, I couldn't help but remember the ecstasy all over again. I was sore, but it was a feeling I'd never known before, and something I definitely wanted to feel again.

With Ryder.

And there lay the problem. Now that he'd stoked my fire, it was going to be difficult to smother the flames. Just thinking about him made my heart beat that bit faster.

I needed to sleep. It was the only way my brain could process all of this and become clear again. I had to shake the sex fog, and become the practical woman I always was.

But it had felt so good to be free.

So good to give myself completely.

So good to be thoroughly fucked by a gorgeous, strong and virile man like Ryder Knox.

Thankful that Mom had just left the tea on my bedside table. I drank it and crawled between the sheets.

A smile came to my lips. I wanted Ryder messing on these Egyptian cotton sheets while fucking me into oblivion.

I needed to find my own place.

Soon.

CHAPTER 6

RYDER

I rolled over and reached for her. How was it possible that it felt like Jade had always belonged here—in my bed? I couldn't get enough of her. Everything about her turned me on: the taste of her skin, her mouth . . . and her pussy. But not only her body and the way she looked—I loved the way her mind worked too. And there was something sweet and caring about her that appealed to me more than I'd want to admit.

But what I loved most, was that my good girl could turn into a naughty girl when she was with me. Yeah.

I wanted to savor her all over again. Fuck, I was getting hard just thinking of where my mouth and dick had been.

Jade wasn't in the bed.

"Babe?" I called out. I knew women went to the bathroom a lot after sex. And we'd been fucking all night long.

No answer. Was Princess playing tricks on me? Or maybe she'd fallen asleep in the bathroom? I wouldn't blame her. It had been a night like no other.

I got up and sauntered to the bathroom, my half-mast dick swinging as I thought of what I was going to do to her when I got her back into the bed. Yeah. My Princess had a fire in her I didn't think I could ever quench. Her greedy pussy just wanted more, no matter how much I'd given her. Next time we were together, I wanted to take her bare. Skin to skin. We needed to have a talk about that . . .

The bathroom was empty. OK. Maybe the balcony? No.

She'd left. *Fuck.*

I wanted to spend more time with her.

I couldn't get enough.

CHAPTER 7

JADE

Spread across the bed, lying on my stomach, and paging through the newspaper, I was looking for rental apartments near Daddy's offices. If I was going to move out, I wanted to be close enough to work so that I didn't spend inordinate amounts of time in traffic jams.

A knock on my door had my head jerking up. Oh shit. *Daddy*. It was time for *the talk*.

"Morning, honey. Can I come in?"

I don't know why he asked, because he was already standing by my bedside, peering over my shoulder at the newspaper. He didn't say anything, he just coughed.

Daddy knows.

He made himself comfortable on my dresser stool, looking very handsome in his tennis outfit. For a man of fifty-three, he was extremely fit. My father went to gym every morning before going to the office, because he believed that a healthy body housed a healthy mind. He also held the opinion that everything was easier if he took his stress out on weights and punching bags.

"Do you want to tell me what happened last night with Marcus? And explain why you went off on a motorcycle and didn't come home until this morning?"

His eyes were hard, belying the smile on his lips. He made me feel like a small child. But this time I was standing up for myself. For far too long, I'd allowed my parents to steer my life.

I sat up, folding my legs underneath me. It was going to be hard to convince him to let me make my own mistakes and also that I needed the freedom to make my own choices—whatever they were.

Because I knew that part of living was to experience pain and loss and hurt. That was the only way to also know happiness and gratitude and live a full life.

As I relayed what'd happened, he sucked in a breath, his jaw setting as he clenched his teeth. Edward Summers was not a man anyone messed with.

Both Harrison and I had inherited his tenacious characteristics. Right now, I wouldn't want to be Marcus.

"Tell me about the man you left with—on the back of his motorcycle, no less," he demanded. "How do you know him?" The sneer on his face got my hackles up immediately. He was judging Ryder without ever having met him, or knowing anything about him.

Strange how only a few months ago, I would've also pulled my nose up in disgust. But now I knew better. I knew not to judge a person by appearances alone.

"He's the man I met at the agency. The one I told you had rented the house in Beverly Hills. He just happened to be there when I needed him. Kind of my knight on a rumbling horse." I laughed, remembering the awkwardness of it all at the time.

Daddy was less amused. "The rude biker guy? Jade! And you actually got on the back of his motorcycle? I've always warned you about staying away from strangers, but this is even worse." His eyebrows furrowed, and his lips thinned into a grimace.

I rolled my eyes. "Daddy, he's not that bad when you get to know him. He's helping out a friend's family. That says a lot about a man's character."

"But Jade, you were the one who told me how unmannered he was. How you didn't trust his motives for renting the house. Now you've done a flip on that assessment?" His eyebrows raised as he glared at me, not pleased at all.

"I got to know him a little during the house inspections. He's a little rough on the outside, I admit, but underneath that exterior is a good heart."

"Are you hearing yourself? Since when did criminals have good hearts? I don't like this one bit, Jade. I'm not even telling your mother about this conversation—she'd lock you in your room. Besides, you're a qualified lawyer now, you should know better than anyone that leopards don't change their spots."

"Ah, but what if he never was a leopard to begin with?" I countered.

"Don't be smart with me, young lady. I'm looking out for your best interests. Bikers are not suitable for my daughter. It happened once, we'll leave it at that, if you promise not to do it again."

I sucked in a breath. "Daddy. Seriously?"

"Yes. And I know what happened with Marcus is distasteful. He should've been more discreet. But you aren't formally engaged yet, so I will have a very serious talk with him and lay down the law for the future. It won't happen again, I promise you, sweetheart."

My mouth went so dry, I nearly choked. I took a sip of orange juice and eyed my father carefully. "I'm not sure I'm understanding this. Let me see if I've got what you're saying right. You're saying what Marcus did is forgivable, and that you expect me to continue seeing and *marrying* him after your man-to-man talk?"

In all my years I'd never questioned my parents. I knew they had my best interests at heart, and only wanted happiness for both Harrison and myself. And now this? I couldn't believe it.

"Oh, honey, no! The choice will be yours, but maybe it's just a misunderstanding, and you can work things out. And if you still want Marcus, I'll make sure he never repeats his despicable behavior." Daddy leaned forward and placed his hand on my shoulder. His eyes had softened. "Masterton just seemed the perfect man for you. He's going places, he's smart, ambitious and... he can provide well for you."

My breath hitched. "After what Marcus did, I expected you to want to cut his balls off. *Not* give him another chance. And no, I don't want him. I've never been in love with Marcus. I'll admit that he was everything I *thought* I wanted in a man. But he's a cheater. He's not loyal."

I rubbed at the pain in my heart with my fist. Yet I was grateful I'd found out about Marcus before things got more serious. Before I gave him my body like I'd planned to do that fateful night—wanting to see if my heart would follow. But what I'd seen—his dick inside another woman—could never be unseen. If Marcus needed to fuck another girl, he clearly wasn't that into me. Because if he was, he would have waited a few more hours—for me.

"I want a man who wants only me. I've learned that money and status and a pretty house with a white picket fence aren't what I want, after all. I want love. And loyalty. I want to be the center of his universe. My man mustn't even think of wanting another woman. So clearly, Marcus is not what I want."

Daddy pursed his lips. He didn't like what I was saying. I think he'd hoped I'd forgive Marcus and move forward. But how could I be with a man who would only be loyal to me because my father threatened him? No, it had to be his choice to be faithful, *because he wanted to.* Because he had no need for anyone else.

"Jade, just think about it before you make up your mind. Your life can be great if you choose Marcus. He can give you everything you need."

Solemn, I shook my head. "I'd always wondered which was more important. *To love, or to be loved.* Then I came across something that resonated with me. Asking that question is like asking a bird which wing it needs most—its right wing or its left wing."

My father cocked his head and smiled, encouraging me to tell him more. I loved that he was willing to listen to my point of view. My voice was barely above a whisper, I was that choked up.

"The truth is that a bird needs both wings to fly. The answer is balance. That's what I want—to both receive and give love equally. Unconditionally. Completely. Can you understand that?"

Finally I understood what I really wanted. A 'shopping' list of characteristics to tick off didn't ensure my happily-ever-after. It wasn't my mind that had to choose which man I spent the rest of my life with. That was entirely my heart's job. And the man that was making my knees weak wasn't the one my mind would've chosen, not in a million years.

He nodded. "I understand, because that's what Mom and I have always had. But, Jade, choose wisely.

Who you decide to spend your life with impacts on many other levels, too. Once the romance dies, you have to still like one another if it's going to last."

"I get that, Daddy. Which is exactly why I can't be with Marcus. I'd never trust him again."

"So, tell me about the motorcycle man. Is there something I should know?" The way he quirked his eyebrow confirmed that he wasn't too comfortable with this development.

"There's not much to tell. He saved me from Marcus and seriously embarrassing moments; that's all. He's not my type, nor am I his, so there's nothing to worry about." Even as I tried to assure my father, my stomach flipped. The little voice in my head was getting louder. Was I telling him the truth?

I hated telling lies, especially to the two people I trusted most in the world. But I hadn't quite figured it out myself yet. I was still eager to find my own place, even if I never saw Ryder again. It was time for the next step into adulthood.

Were my feelings for Ryder becoming more than just rebellion and lust?

I hope not.

CHAPTER 8

RYDER

"Get into the fucking wheelchair." I nodded my head toward the contraption Cobra was refusing to get into. "I'll wheel you out of this place and take you home. But first, you gotta follow the damn rules."

Cobra's eyes widened. "Fuck. Ryder, is this really you speaking? Since when do you, of all people, follow the rules?"

I winked at him. "Since it's the fastest way to get out of this place that smells like antiseptic and is as sterile as Ox's balls."

He chuckled. "You got a point, brother. Get me the fuck outta here."

Cobra leaned on both the nurse and myself as we lowered him into the wheelchair. He grinned like a fool up at the nurse. "Don't go missing me too much, sweetheart."

She swatted him with the clipboard. "Get your ugly

mug out of here before you have another injury. And stay out of the way of bullets in future, will you?" She quirked an eyebrow at him.

I laughed. "Trouble is Cobra's middle name. Follows him like a stench."

The nurse placed a few containers of painkillers in Cobra's hands and explained how he should take them. He listened patiently, and nodded his head. Fuck, was Cobra going soft after all this time in the hospital? The Cobra I knew would have chucked the pills in the bin, proclaiming to be a man, and not a pussy who needed pills to get through the pain.

We were inside the elevator when Cobra spoke again. "Mia?" His voice was so soft that I hardly heard it. I even detected anxiety. Yeah. When a woman had a man by the balls, there was no way he could pretend otherwise. He was fucked, whether he knew it or not.

"Mia's at the house. Waiting for you. Don't stress too much, she was dolling herself up when I left. She can't be that mad at you if she wants to look all pretty for you."

"Yeah?" Cobra sighed. "Since when are you such a fucking expert on women? Thought you hated bitches, except for their pussies."

I shook with laughter. "Since looking after *your* old lady. Babysitting *your* family. And since—" I stopped talking just in time. Cobra didn't know anything about Jade. Was bad enough that Mia was constantly interrogating me. I didn't need him on my case, too.

Besides, since I'd last seen her that night, she hadn't been taking my calls. She was being stubborn as hell, sticking to her guns. But what Jade didn't know was that besides being a tenacious man, I was also a patient fucker. *If it suited me.*

"You were saying?"

"Nothing, man. Just glad you're out of this place. Gives me the creeps."

"Ryder. I'm your brother. No secrets. If you don't tell me, Mia will. You know that woman knows everything."

"It's complicated. Let it go, brother. Focus on Mia and the kids. Excited to see them?"

"Hell yeah. I'm sure they've grown so much since I last saw them."

"They have. Your family is really awesome. You're a lucky man, Cobra."

"How lucky? I'll find out when I see Mia again. You know she's not gonna forgive me easily for losing the baby. And I don't blame her, either."

Silently, I nodded. Losing a baby was a big deal. One score I hadn't settled yet with the fucking LA Demons. That baby's premature death was on them. Fuckers.

"Anyway, stay at the 'Rental Ritz' in Beverly Hills, as Mia and I call it, for a few weeks while you get stronger. Take the time to bond with Mia, to sort your shit. 'Cause once you get back to the club, you gotta step back into your pres shoes. Razor has been doing a stellar job of keeping the club running, if you know what I mean. With both you and me gone, he's been king of the fucking world."

"Little bastard must be having a ball. Nobody to rein him in. Has he been up to any shit?"

We reached the black SUV with the heavily tinted windows. I quickly ran a scan to make sure nobody had tampered with it since I left it in the car park. Those fuckers were still out to kill us, so I had to be sure.

"There's this new barmaid chick, Lexi. Between Ox and Razor, I think she's getting royally fucked. Neither man will give way to the other. We may have shit on our hands."

"And you? Have you got stuck into the bitch, too?"

"Nah. Not my type." I lifted Cobra out of the wheelchair and put him on the back seat. Fuck, he'd lost so much weight. I lifted him easily. I'd never been able to do that before.

"Since when has a pussy not been your type? You fuck any pussy—especially fresh pussy. Want to tell me why not this one?"

"I've been at the house, remember? Doing your fucking job, looking after your family."

"Some other pussy has gotten to you. Fuck, how did I miss that?"

"You're blowing smoke, man. That ain't true."

"Jesus. You've got it bad, brother. Nothing has ever stopped you from taking pussy at the club, even if other men were in there too. You can't fucking bluff, Ryder. 'Cause I've been there, brother. Since I laid eyes on Mia, I didn't want any other pussy. Only hers. You're cunt-struck. and you ain't telling me."

"Fuck off, Cobra. It's none of your business."

Cobra pulled a face as I strapped him in. "Mia will know. She'll fill me in."

"Mia knows nothing. I ain't telling you or her my business."

"Fuck. Ryder, what is it with your bitch?" He paused for a moment and I could feel his gaze burning into me. "Must be something if you won't talk to me. Or Mia. Something fucking serious."

I got behind the wheel and closed my eyes. Cobra wouldn't let this go till I told him about Jade and her brother. And I knew what he'd say. He'd tell me to back the fuck off. He wouldn't understand that I couldn't. My mind and my cock wouldn't let go of Jade, even if I knew she was dangerous territory.

"Yeah. There's this woman—"

"I fucking knew it!" Cobra sounded triumphant. "So why hide it, Ryder? It ain't no sin to want a bitch, brother. Even happened to me." He chuckled, as if he were still surprised by it happening to him.

"Well, this one is different. Not only is she a fucking princess, her brother is a cop. Special Task Forces cop. And her daddy's a criminal lawyer. Beat that for fucked up." I sighed. "And even worse, she doesn't want anything to do with me. She says it can't work out. Family, and all that shit."

Cobra let out a long breath, whistling through his teeth. "Fuck, Ryder. Can't you ever just do simple?" He leaned back against the seat and closed his eyes.

After a minute he talked softly. "How bad do you want this bitch?"

"Bad. Give both my balls bad."

"Christ. You're fucked."

"Yeah. I know."

CHAPTER 9

RYDER

As we stopped in the driveway of the house, Mia came out to greet her husband. I frowned, annoyed that the woman hadn't listened to me. I got out of the SUV and went to get Cobra's door.

Mia spoke softly behind me. "Ryder. I know you said not to come out. But I can't help myself. I miss Cobra so much."

"I know. Wait inside the back door. I need to help him in. He won't want you to see that. Go." My voice was harsher than I meant it to be, but it was dangerous for us to be outside, anyone could have followed us. And I had my hands full helping Cobra; I didn't need to still worry about Mia's safety too. Cobra was a huge fucker—even though he'd lost weight, I still needed all my strength to lift him out of the SUV.

"Thanks, brother. Saving a man's dignity." Cobra patted me on the back as I lifted him. Yeah, a man always wanted to appear tough and strong in front of his woman. She had to believe he could protect her at all times. Showing weakness was not an option, especially not for a man like Cobra, who believed in the laws of the jungle: survival of the fittest.

"No problem, brother." I set him down and helped him get inside by supporting his body with my arm.

"Baby," he breathed when his gaze landed on Mia.

"Cobra. I'm so glad you're here, baby." Mia's voice cracked.

She slid an arm around his waist and stood on tiptoes to kiss him. So far it all seemed good. Between us, we helped the enormous man to the main bedroom. Sweat was pouring from his face due to exertion. There was still a long way to go for my best friend before he'd be back to his old self, but every day he got better, and that was something to be grateful for. I didn't know what I would've done if the bastard had gotten killed that day.

"The kids?" Cobra asked.

Mia spoke softly as she wiped Cobra's forehead. "I called Jade. She's taken them to the new Disney movie. Gives us time to settle you in and talk."

"Jade? Who's Jade? Is it safe for the kids to be out with a fucking stranger?" Cobra growled. Yeah, he was getting better.

"Jade's a friend. She's the rental agent. She's totally safe, and very cute. In fact, I think Ryder is sweet on her."

Cobra's gaze shot to me, his eyebrows lifted to his hairline. Fuck. Back in the house less than two minutes and Mia already told Cobra. Plus, after what I'd told him in the car, I'd never fucking live it down.

"Yeah? That true, Ryder?"

"Nah, she's just a piece of ass. Mia should know me

by now—I don't get attached to bitches. Ever."

"Really, Ryder? That's why you brought her here the other night. Don't think I don't know she slept here." She cleared her throat. "Not much sleep going on, but you know what I mean."

I grimaced. "Mia. That's how you thank a brother for taking care of you and your babies? By ratting on him the first chance you get?"

"Cobra's going to see the spark between the two of you the minute Jade gets here with the kids. Anyone would have to be blind to not know the two of you are crazy for one another." She turned to Cobra. "But they're both so stubborn, baby. Neither will admit it. Jade says it's too complicated with her family. Ryder has a hard-on the minute he sees her, but tries to pretend otherwise." She laughed, sounding happy for the first time in weeks.

Grumbling, I left the bedroom and closed the door behind me. They needed their privacy—they had a shitload of stuff to talk about. And I definitely didn't want to discuss Jade with Cobra.

Stripping down to my boxers, I jumped straight into the pool and swam a few laps. The water was refreshing, and I enjoyed the strain of working my muscles. I dried myself off and I lazed around on one of those fancy reclining chairs I'd always seen rich people sip cocktails in. It was the first time in weeks that I just had a bit of time to myself, and lying in the sun after a swim was something I could get used to.

I must've dozed off. Jamie had climbed on top of me and stroked my cheek to wake me. Startled, I sat up, looking straight into those fucking blue eyes that haunted my dreams. Jade was back with the kids. With the sun behind her head, it looked as if she wore a halo. Her blond hair shone in the bright light, and her lips gleamed as she pouted them while looking down at me.

Standing with Isabella on her hip, her legs were parted, and with the sunlight behind her, I could see right through the flimsy material. Fuck me, if she wasn't wearing a bright pink lacey thong. The silhouette of her legs through the thin fabric, long and perfect, made my dick jump.

Jesus.

"Hello, Ryder," she drawled before her face split into a smile. God, it was the most beautiful smile I'd ever seen. Was Mia right? Was I going soft on Princess? Yeah, I wanted to fuck her all right. I was always up for that with *any* bitch. But never before had I been affected by a fucking *smile.* I hadn't realized just how much I'd missed the beautiful bitch until her sweet face appeared in front of me.

She raised an eyebrow, and stared at my boxers. Yep, my erection stood proud, and tented the satin fabric. She was lucky I was even wearing goddamn boxers. I wanted to drag her to my room and fuck the daylight out of her.

Instead I just grunted, and placed a towel over my stomach, laying my hard cock flat on my belly. Her laugh was sweet and sexy. She knew she did this to me.

"*Batman?*"

"Was a birthday gift from one of the boys," I explained. She hadn't seen the others yet. I had the whole fucking Marvel comic club in my underwear drawer, compliments of the guys trying to be funny.

"It's cute. Goes with your tattoos."

Cute? What the fuck was she talking about? I was mean and angry. Never cute.

"Anyway, I'm just dropping the kids. Got to go." The smile that had warmed my heart had faded, and she had that serious look in her eyes. *Fuck.*

"Stay. Let's get a drink first. I'm sure the kids are thirsty. What do you say, Jamie, my man? Should Jade have a drink with us before she goes?"

Jamie always came through for me. He nodded his head vigorously. How could she refuse the kid? I was bargaining on that, knowing she wouldn't stay for me.

"OK. Just a juice, then I have to leave."

"Juice it is," I said, happy that she'd be around a while longer.

I watched her ass as she swayed her hips, walking toward the house. Man, I could so get into that ass right now. Pulling on my jeans, I swallowed the lump in my throat as I followed her, grateful that she couldn't see my hard-on still raging for her.

Just as we finished drinking our juice, Mia came to the kitchen.

"I heard the car. Thanks for taking the kids, Jade. Cobra wants to see them now." She took Isabella from Jade's arms, and took Jamie by the hand. "I owe you one, Jade. You're a sweetheart."

Jade flashed Mia a smile. "It's my pleasure. Happy to help out at any time."

We watched Mia and the kids for a moment as they left the room.

"I have to go now," Jade said, avoiding my eyes.

"Princess."

I blocked her path, pulling her to my chest.

"Ryder. Don't."

Her eyes darted to the door.

"They won't be back for a while. Relax." Dipping my head, I whispered into her ear. "Bet you're wet for me. You know I'm already hard for you."

It had only been a few days since I'd seen Jade, yet I was desperate for her. I'd jerked off a few times in the mornings, and also in the evenings before falling asleep, imagining her tits swinging above my face and the feel of her wet cunt, but it wasn't the same as the real thing. I needed to get inside her. Now. For real.

Did Jade feel the same?

I walked her backward and pushed her ass against the counter, grinding my hardness into her. She groaned. My lips found the soft, warm skin under her ear and nibbled gently.

My hand snuck under her dress, targeting that fucking bright-pink thong. She'd worn them under a white dress on purpose—to drive my cock wild. I felt the dampness of the scrap of lace. She was fucking soaked.

"Spread your legs," I ordered.

I bit softly into her neck as my fingers found their way under the fabric and into her wetness. "You need my fucking cock, don't you?"

She didn't answer. I jammed two fingers into her, gauging her readiness. She was more than ready. Her head rolled backward as I slowly finger-fucked her.

She whimpered as I gripped a handful of hair and pulled hard, staring into her glazed eyes. "Princess. Tell me you need my cock."

Her voice was barely above a whisper. "I need you."

"Tell me you need my cock. *Beg* for it."

"Ryder," she moaned.

"Tell me you wore these pink panties for me. So I would fuck you."

"I did. I wore them for you. I knew they'd please you."

"Ahh, you beautiful slut, I knew you did," I crooned triumphantly. "Now tell me how much you need my cock to fuck you."

I stuck a third finger into her, massaging her G-spot. She bit her lip, her hands gripping the counter, her knuckles white.

"I won't let you come till you beg me."

Her breath came in small spurts. She was close. "Ryder, please. I need your cock. Inside. Fucking me." Her voice was hoarse, and sexy as hell.

Jesus Christ.

She'd turned the tables on me, and just like that, I wasn't the one in control. I had to get inside that pussy. Now.

Turning her around to face the counter, I pushed her cheek to the cool marble.

"Hold on." I pulled my jeans and boxers down and quickly rolled on a condom. We needed to talk about that. I didn't want latex between us again.

I leaned down and pulled her panties down her legs. "Step out," I commanded. I needed these for later. I was keeping them.

My cock slid into her and I sighed, kissing her neck. My hands found her tits and squeezed as I slipped my cock in and out of her.

I pulled hard on her nipples, wanting to make her cry out. I had to punish her for making me want her so much that I ached all over when she was gone, and even more when she was close. She was my drug. Princess had hooked me with her smart mouth and sweet pussy. I couldn't get enough, and now she had to pay for that.

"God, Ryder. Harder," she groaned, pushing her ass backward.

Fuck. She was enjoying it.

I gripped her throat and squeezed, my free hand slipping to her clit and strumming it with my thumb while I held her body down against the cold countertop with my weight.

Jade was mine. I owned her. I owned her pussy and her orgasm.

Princess couldn't scream my name out loud with the others in the house. But the way her body shook, I knew she would've if I didn't keep her quiet.

"Grip my cock with your pussy. Make me come," croaked as I rode her at breakneck speed, fucking her hard, my balls slapping against her perfect ass.

She did. Her pussy milked my cock as she rode her orgasm, gasping for air as I possessed her completely, even controlling how much air she breathed.

Jesus. This woman was perfect. Perfect for me.

CHAPTER 10

JADE

Back home in my bed, I ran earlier events through my head again. After I'd succumbed so easily to Ryder, against my better judgment, I knew I had to get out of there as fast as possible, or I'd end up in his bed—again.

Mia and the kids stayed in the main bedroom with Cobra—I'd heard the kids laughing and chattering. It would be a while before they were ready to share their time with anyone outside their close little family unit.

I hadn't planned on seeing Ryder, although, in all honesty, I was hoping he'd be there. My disappointment at not seeing him when I picked up the kids made me decide not to get my hopes up, just in case he wasn't around when I returned. It was my lucky day when I found him lazing by the pool. He was like honey, and I was the bee—I couldn't have resisted him even if I'd tried.

Tossing around in my bed, I knew I had to explain

to Ryder why I couldn't keep on seeing him. That it wasn't because I was a snob or looked down on him. *Because I didn't any longer.* Shame washed over me as I remembered how I'd treated Ryder when I'd first met him. He was right—I'd acted like a bitch. But I had reasons.

Good reasons. One of them was because of my dear brother. My heart squeezed when I thought of him.

There was nothing cheerful about Harrison Summers. The permanent scowl on his handsome face only softened when he was at home, around me, and our parents. I loved Harrison with all my heart—he was the best brother a girl could wish for. Except that he was overbearingly protective, ever since the day of *The Incident.*

It took years of therapy to shake the guilt that it was my fault, and that I was to blame that Harrison was like this. Although it took place nearly ten years ago, whenever I had a flashback, it was as vivid as if it had happened only yesterday.

Ryder insisting on being in my life had brought on just such a flashback. I sat up, bewildered, images rushing through my brain.

No, please, I don't want to remember . . .

Huddled against the headboard, my knees drawn to my chest, I rocked myself as tears streamed freely down my cheeks.

*****

Harrison kissed Amy and swatted her on the ass. "Go ahead with the others, babe. Get into the long line at the entrance. We don't want to be late for the concert. Jade and I will catch up."

He turned to me and laughed. "Hurry, Sis, you're going to make us late. Go get your sweater—I'll wait right here for you." I was always losing stuff and luckily Harrison was patient with me. Love for my big brother surged through me—he knew me so well.

I nodded and ran back into the fast-food restaurant to get the sweater I'd accidentally left behind. It was my favorite; I'd be crushed if I lost it. Besides, it usually got cold in the evenings, and at outdoor events and I'd need it to keep me warm. Harrison and his other friends had girlfriends to cuddle with if they were cold. I was alone.

It was my first live concert, and adrenaline spiked my bloodstream—I didn't want to miss a second of Karma Electric, they were my favorite band. I swiped up my sweater from where it had dropped on the floor.

I was lucky my parents had agreed to let me go to the event with Harrison on a week night, so I didn't want to spoil his evening. And I'd hoped Harrison would invite me again the next time he and his buddies went to a rock concert. Those were the perks of having an older brother. My friends at school were all jealous that I'd get to see the dreamy new lead singer of the band before they did.

"Got it?" Harrison shot me an impatient glance as he crushed the cigarette with his foot. I never knew my brother smoked till tonight.

"Yeah. Sorry. It was on the floor."

"Put it on before you drop it again."

Harrison chuckled as he watched Amy blow him a kiss, and tore his gaze away from the little group halfway across the large opening to help me dutifully into my sweater.

Gunshots rang out.

Both our heads jerked toward the ominous sound. What we saw would scar us for life. Both of Harrison's friends and their girlfriends were mowed down, including Amy. I screamed so loudly that I couldn't hear

Harrison's words to me, but his expression told me to stay put. I couldn't have moved if I tried to, I was frozen to the spot. Pandemonium broke out around me. People were screaming hysterically, and running around blindly. I watched Harrison run across the patch of grass, reaching Amy just as the cops did.

Amy and the other four were caught in the crossfire between a biker gang and the police. Four were dead, and one survived. One of his friends, Michael, got shot in the knees, and fell down before more bullets could kill him.

Amy had been shot through the heart, and died minutes later in Harrison's arms.

It was biker bullets that killed Amy and Harrison's friends. With little regard for the lives of others, they'd shot at the cops who'd recognized them.

Harrison wanted to die. Said he should have been there with Amy. That if he had his arm around her, she may still have been alive. I shuddered at the thought—it would've meant my brother would be dead.

If it weren't for me, both Harrison and I would've been with the group, but we may have been further along, avoiding the crossfire altogether. All it took was a few seconds to be in the wrong place at the wrong time. It was ALL my fault.

I should've been dead.

And Harrison wished he was.

Even now, after all these years.

*****

The images had faded somewhat over time, but my heart was still breaking for the loss of those innocent young lives. I rubbed at my heart, trying to lessen the physical pain. Life would've been so different if that hadn't happened.

From that day on, Harrison had hated bikers. He'd made it his life's mission to stamp out biker clubs and crimes associated with them. Cleaning up the streets and banning groups of bikers from public places was what he dreamed about, because he never wanted an incident like that to repeat itself on innocent victims.

I got that.

Hell, I was on his side. We both recognized the gangster type immediately and had a strong aversion to anyone who was a biker in a MC. They were the scum of the earth.

Until Ryder.

Until I met a man who outwardly portrayed every one of those traits. I should hate him and his kind for what they did to Amy and the others. For what they did to me, and to Harrison.

Yet I couldn't hate Ryder. Underneath that hardened exterior was just a man, one who had his own burdens weighing him down. Who the hell was I to judge him and his kind? I knew nothing of their pain or their reasons for being what they were.

But how could I explain that to Harrison? He wouldn't even listen. For as stubborn as I was, Harrison was tenfold more so.

My head hurt from all the thinking. I had to get through to Ryder that we could never see one another again. That what had happened on the back of his bike and in the kitchen were a moment-of-madness mistake we couldn't allow to be repeated.

My heart ached. It was going to be the hardest thing I'd ever done—to deny myself the feelings that flooded my being when I thought about Ryder Knox.

He felt them too—I didn't need a crystal ball to know that. Ryder never apologized for telling me blatantly just how much he wanted me, in every carnal and lustful way. There was a magnetism we couldn't deny, a pull stronger than logic permitted. We were so different, yet we fitted so well together. It was beyond reasoning. Beyond anything I'd ever imagined. Not even the romance novels I consumed could have prepared me for this.

But I had to sacrifice my feelings of lust for Ryder because there no good could come of it. We were doomed from the start.

I. Had. To. Choose. My. Family.

Why had Ryder chosen Clarke and Sons Agency that day?

And why in hell could he not just let go? Move on?

And why, oh why was I so drawn to him, so weak when it came to resisting him?

Why?

Still bewildered by my emotions, I became aware of a strange noise. It reminded me of when I was a teen-ager and boys threw pebbles against my window. Then it dawned on me—that was exactly what it was. I scooted off the bed to the window as another pebble hit it smack in the middle of the glass. What little delinquent was pranking me at this time of the night?

I pushed the window open and gasped. Ryder was standing there in the darkness, a lopsided grin on his handsome face. *Fuck.* This was worse than when I was a teenager. Back then I was too innocent to know better. A boy beneath my window sent my heart aflutter. Now other parts of me were fluttering, way down south from my heart.

"Let me in," he demanded, his arms folded over his chest.

"Shhh," I gestured, then shook my head.

"Fine," he muttered and walked away. What? Was

he giving up that easily? He disappeared out of sight around the corner, without any further protest. I was pretty disappointed, but it was better this way. I didn't want him to see that I'd been crying. I wiped my nose with my sleeve and crawled back in to bed.

I closed my eyes, confused even more. Why had Ryder come here? Why had he left without even trying? Was he finally listening to me? And did I really want him to?

"Fuck, Princess. You're killing me." Ryder stood in my doorway, his silhouette in the dark visible by the light of the moon. *Was I dreaming?*

"Ryder! W . . . what? H . . . how?" I switched on the bedside lamp.

"If you won't let me in, I'll let myself in." He grinned, his gaze raking appreciatively up my semi-naked body. I was wearing only a tee and panties.

"But . . . but the doors are locked . . . and we have alarms . . ." Had Daddy forgotten to lock up?

Ryder chuckled softly. "Babe, nothing will stop me if I want to get in somewhere. Breaking in is an undervalued skill, and definitely one of my many talents." He wiggled his eyebrows at me.

"Yeah? And did you poison the Rottweiler?" Mom had insisted on having a trained guard dog. It made her feel safer. Bruno was alert and fierce, yet I hadn't heard him growl or bark as he usually did when strangers came to the house.

"The pup and I are friends. I'm definitely not going to be his breakfast." He sat on the bed, watching me.

My eyes widened. Bruno was a muscled brute of a dog; he hadn't been a puppy in five years. How had Ryder gotten past Bruno? He didn't take kindly to strangers.

"*Princess*. You've been crying—tell me why." His

voice was hoarse, yet soft.

My throat was still thick, and tears sat just behind my eyelids, ready to spring forth again. I couldn't speak. I wanted Ryder here more than anything, but I also wanted him to leave, for his own sake. I was so confused.

"Baby," he said softly as he pulled me to his chest.

God it felt good. And the way he said the word *baby*, with the slightest dip in his voice as if he were affected too, made it sound sexy and comforting at the same time. My breath hitched—he'd called me baby—not babe, not bitch, not Princess. *Just baby*. And I loved it.

I let him hold me, let him stroke my back, soothing me while he hummed. This was a side of the tough, badass biker I doubted anyone had ever seen. Was he even aware he was doing it?

"Why did you come?" I whispered, my breath catching as I spoke.

"I'll tell you . . . if you tell me why you're crying," he countered.

I fell silent for a long time, organizing my thoughts. Ryder kept rubbing my back, placing no pressure on me but waiting patiently for me to reply.

At last I spoke. It was as if the floodgates opened. I told him the whole story. *Everything.*

Ryder listened, only grunting occasionally, his fingers making small circular motions up and down my spine. I inhaled deeply, drawing his scent into my nostrils and basking in his warm embrace. He'd comforted me and lulled me into a relaxed state.

"Um, Ryder?"

"Yes, baby?"

"Now I've told you the whole story—why did you come?"

He was quiet for the longest time, but never resting

his fingers. "Because I needed to be near you. Because I can never get enough of you. That's why."

He shifted down the bed, holding me in his arms. My head rested on his chest, listening to the rhythmic beat of his heart.

"Sleep baby, I'll hold you. It's all OK. That shit happened a long time ago. None of it was your fault. None. You gotta let that go. OK?"

Drowsy, I nodded my head. It felt like a huge weight had been lifted off my shoulders. Why, I wasn't sure. All I'd done, was tell Ryder my and Harrison's story; the story I'd hidden deep inside for so long, trying to bury it. Yet now that I'd set it free, it no longer weighed as heavily on me.

Ryder had done for me what no therapist ever could. He'd gotten me to set the ugly past free. He'd even gotten me to start believing that maybe it wasn't my fault after all. I sighed as he kissed the crown of my head, a shudder of utter relief running through my body, letting the tension flow away.

"Go to sleep. I'm here now." His voice was like velvet, soft and soothing. Hypnotic. I drifted off into a peaceful sleep with Ryder holding me, feeling safe and secure.

Pure bliss.

CHAPTER 11

RYDER

"Are you sure you're up to this, brother?" I quirked an eyebrow at Cobra who was all dressed except for his cut, ready to go back to the compound for the first time since the shootout.

"Yeah. It's time to sort out club business. Take my place at the gavel. Work out what we're going to do."

Cobra was stubborn. It made him the badass man he was. He never gave up, and he never gave in. OK, except to Mia. And his babies. But never to another man. Tough as fucking nails, he went head-to-head with his enemies.

We made small talk for most of the journey, both of us with our minds wandering elsewhere. So when we fell into a comfortable silence we just let it be, allowing ourselves the small pleasure of being lost in our own thoughts, without interruption.

I was between a rock and a hard place. I was falling

for Jade, yet I knew her brother would string me up the first chance he got. Now that I'd finally gotten the story out of her, I wasn't bitter or vengeful about his motives. Fuck, if that'd happened to me, I would've hunted the motherfuckers down and killed them with my bare fucking hands.

A part of me even respected the guy for wanting to protect his little sister. Remembering back to what I was willing to sacrifice to save Max's life, I understood how Harrison Summers felt about Jade. Fuck, if it weren't for our pasts, we could probably even have been friends.

But that wouldn't stop me from putting a bullet in his skull if he threatened my family. Fuck, if he hurt any one of my brothers at the Scorpio Stinger MC I'd have to take him down. It was the code of our brotherhood. It was simply the way it worked, regardless of who the fucker was who tried to take a brother down.

Sighing heavily, I pulled up at the compound, in front of the heavy gates and pressed the button to let us in. While we waited, I couldn't help noticing how derelict the warehouse was. Our headquarters appeared deserted. Usually there were bikes and people everywhere, but since the shootout, everyone kept cover as much as they could. We'd even built a fucking shed for the bikes so they could be locked up at night, ensuring nobody tampered with them. Yeah, we had to cover all our bases.

The gloomy clubhouse was in desperate need of restoration. Peeling paint and bullet holes in the walls had never bothered me before. I guess I'd been so used to its appearance that it'd seemed normal. Now it was depressing. Maybe it was because I'd been living in the fancy part of town for a while that I'd become aware of the stark contrast. *Funny the things we get accustomed to.*

This was not the day to help Cobra out of the SUV. Even though he struggled, sweat trickling down his forehead as he contorted his face in agony, I watched him get down the step by himself. Cobra was the pres of Scorpio Stinger MC, for fuck's sake. He needed to maintain the respect of all the brothers. Show that a few bullets wouldn't stop him.

Suppressing the urge to put my arm around Cobra to support him, I walked to the door to hold it open. But before I could even reach the door, brothers came pouring out into the square to welcome their pres. The place that appeared so desolate moments before was transformed by all the familiar faces. The shouting and whistling startled me; I'd forgotten what a rowdy bunch these guys were.

Backslapping and brother-hugging with roars of laughter was a sure sign that everyone was relieved to have Cobra back at the helm. Yeah, it felt good to be home. I'd missed this place and these faces more than I cared to admit. Here, within these walls, I was just Ryder, a brother, like everyone else. It felt good to belong.

Ox lifted Cobra into his bulging arms, carrying him like a baby.

"Fuck, Pres, what have those people outside been feeding you? Rabbit food? Lettuce leaves ain't for biker boys. We gonna get a steak into you and feed you up."

If I didn't know better I'd think that Ox fucking teared up, because he nearly choked on his last words.

"Yeah. And beer. Get Pres a fucking beer," Ratbag piped up.

It was nine am, but that had never stopped the boys before, and today they had reason for celebration. Cobra let it go. He reveled in the attention, and knew his boys needed something to take their minds off the last few months. In time we'd get to the serious stuff, the business end of club matters. But for now, it was beer all 'round.

Inside the clubhouse, Lexi was sliding one frothy glass after another across the counter like a pro. I had to admit I was impressed.

"Never seen a Sheila pull a beer so fast—she's a fucking natural." Ratbag laughed when he saw the puzzled look on my face. Wasn't her name Lexi? "Yeah, *Sheila* is what we call bitches back in Australia."

Ratbag never failed to amuse me with his strange way of talking and turns of phrases.

"Oi, Sheila, get our VP a beer, sweetheart," he shouted at her.

Lexi didn't slide the beer across the counter to me like she did for the other guys. "You still owe me a visit from last time." She winked as she handed me a beer, leaning over so I could see down her top and making damn sure her hand touched mine. She pouted her full lips and I had that feeling of déjà vu. I could swear I'd seen her somewhere, *before* she worked at the club as the barmaid.

Perplexed, I turned away and made a toast to Cobra, welcoming him back and wishing him a speedy recovery so that he'd be one hundred percent fit again.

Downing my beer, I was eager to escape to my room down the hallway. I hadn't slept at the club in months, and I was feeling kinda homesick. I unlocked the door and grinned: everything was exactly as I'd left it. Even my old guitar. Yeah. I hadn't played in forever. As I ran a finger over the strings, I heard the door close behind me.

Whirling around, my hand went for my gun.

"Hey, slow down cowboy, it's only me." Lexi leaned against the door, giving me her best come-fuck-me look.

"Sheila, shouldn't you be working the bar?" I growled. I knew exactly why she was here.

"You can call me anything you want to, Ryder. But my name is Lexi. That's the name to call out when I suck your cock and you come in my mouth."

She pushed away from the door and knelt down in front of me. She ran her fingers over the guitar, slowly, suggestively, never taking her eyes off mine. I hadn't had a bitch that was so overt in her intentions in a while.

I stared down at her, feeling my cock stir. Christ, I was only a man.

Lexi took hold of the ends of her skimpy top and pulled it over her head. Her tits were spectacular. Big brown nipples stood hard, already aroused. I watched as she licked her fingertips and started rolling her nipples between her fingers, moaning softly as she bit her bottom lip. She sat back on her knees and ran one hand down her ribs and over her thigh. She pushed up her skirt to her hips and exposed a glistening pussy with the smallest of landing strips covering her mound. Two fingers dipped into her cunt, pushing in deep as she groaned and then removed her fingers.

"Sweet, Ryder. Fucking sweet. Want to taste, baby?" She held her fingers up to my face.

Fuck. My cock went hard. I could smell the bitch from here. She was dripping sex.

When I didn't react, she sucked her fingers into her mouth, tasting herself.

Fuck. That's hot.

Groaning, I placed my hand on her head as she unbuckled my belt and pulled the zipper down. She reached in and set my erection free, her hand on my shaft.

"Hello, Mister." She chuckled, pleased with my

reaction to her.

Her tongue snaked out to lick my cock. Just as she was about to make contact, I pushed her backward so that she fell flat on her naked ass.

"Sheila. A few ground rules. One. You only touch my cock when invited to. Two. If I want to fuck you, I will let you know. Till then, you wait."

"Jesus. What's wrong with you? I've been saving myself for you. Half the club's guys are eager to sink their dicks into me. But I don't want them—I want you. Your cock *likes* me, baby. Don't be a hard-ass."

"Don't call me 'baby,'" I snapped, shoving my semi-hard dick back into my jeans. I ran a hand through my hair. She was right. What the fuck was wrong with me? What man in his right mind would deny himself a pussy like this one? *Sheila* had one fine pussy. Her body was tight, her tits were to die for, and her eagerness to please was every man's dream.

Ahhh. There lay the problem. Because the face in *my* dreams was a *different* face. Similar features, same hot, tight body, but the blue eyes of an angel that tormented my cock with just her smile. *Jade*. Fucking Princess had invaded my mind. She owned my fucking cock, and she didn't even know it. Neither had I, until this very fucking moment. If anyone was going to suck my cock, the mouth had to belong to my Princess.

Lexi gasped. "You've fallen for somebody, haven't you?"

"What the fuck are you? A witch? Get out of my room. Now."

Where the fuck had I seen this bitch before?

I leaned against the wall as she grabbed her top. *Tempting.* Those tits were so fucking tempting. All I had to do was reach out and touch them. Suck those nipples into my mouth. Finger her juicy pussy. Let her suck my cock. Bend her over and fuck her hard.

Why not?

Jade would never know.

But I would.

Even though I was a man—one who loved fucking pussy—it hit me.

I only wanted one pussy. Jade's.

Fuck.

CHAPTER 12

RYDER

"You're making a big mistake, Ryder. I can make you a very happy man." She gestured toward her body with a sweep of her hand. "I will fuck you any way you want. You will love me calling you baby. My pussy is so ready for you Ryder, so wet, throbbing for your cock."

Taking a few steps toward me, she pushed her still naked tits against me. Her hard nipples pushed into my chest. She took hold of my hand and placed it on her sex, spreading her legs.

"Look into my eyes and tell me you don't want my wet cunt. Tell me you don't want to eat me out and be inside me now, and I'll walk away. But you can't, can you?"

Lexi's hand was on my dick, stroking my hardness through the denim. It responded by growing even more.

"Jesus, Sheila. You're one bad bitch. If it weren't for Princess, I'd fuck you till you passed out. But my dick has an affinity for another pussy. Sorry darling," I said as I pushed her onto the bed with a hard shove and walked from the room without looking back.

Fuck, if I stayed another minute I'd be tappin' that ass so hard. I barely could stop myself from taking what was on offer. Sheila would be an awesome fuck. If it weren't for Jade...

"Who the fuck is *Princess*? I'll kill that bitch!" she called from my room.

The roar of my laughter echoed off the hallway walls—Sheila sure was spunky. I shook my head. Now that'd be one showdown I didn't want to be part of. If Jade saw the half-naked dripping-with-sex slut in my room—if she'd seen her hand on my cock, her tits pushed against me, my hands on her pussy—I'd fear for Sheila's life.

And mine. Yeah.

It wasn't official with me and Jade. Not yet. But I knew as much as I'd rip any cockhead apart that tried to fuck Jade, she'd do the same for me. Jesus. Just the thought of another man touching *my Princess*, had steam coming from my ears.

So no, I wasn't tappin' that ass, no matter how tempting, or how horny I felt. Because if I wanted the same behavior from Jade, I had to give her that, too. If there was one thing I never fucked with it was Karma. Because yeah, that bitch had a way of leveling things that us humans had no idea about.

I needed a fucking beer. Pronto.

"Where you been, brother?" Cobra asked as I got back to the clubroom.

"Just to check my room was OK." I pulled a beer and virtually gulped it down in one go.

"Something happen there?" Cobra raised an eyebrow. Brother was sharp. He knew me so well that it was scary as fuck.

"Nah. All good," I said as I downed the last drop and went to get another for Cobra and myself.

"Where the hell is the barmaid? Isn't that her fucking job?" Cobra complained as he nodded toward the bar. He was grumpy as fuck. I knew he was in pain and had to get back to resting soon.

"Yeah, where is she?" Razor asked as he looked around. The look on his face was thunderous. Jesus, if I'd fucked Sheila, I'd have my dick cut off by more than only Jade. Razor had it bad for the girl. And she said she'd been saving herself for me? This was some fucked-up shit. I smelled trouble brewing. If Razor hadn't been able to get to that pussy, I was assuming neither had Ox or any of the other boys. And she was offering it to me on a platter? Since when did I get so fucking lucky? I smirked, and drank more beer.

This morning on our way here, I'd contemplated moving back to the clubhouse. I was going to talk it over with Cobra on the way home. Now I wasn't so sure it was a good idea.

Resisting temptation seemed futile, 'cause I knew the kind of woman Lexi was—she was going to try everything till she had my cock inside her pussy. She was the black-widow type of woman—she'd lure her prey, and then eat him afterwards. Usually that kind of game amused me. The sex was intense, borderline deadly.

A few months ago, I would've taken Lexi—I still thought the name Sheila suited her better—till I tired of her, and then passed her on to the brothers. I wouldn't have cared less about anybody's feeling as long as I was satisfied having that fine ass to myself. A few weeks or so, and I'd have had my fill of her. Because once I mastered her, got her tamed, the game ended. It always did.

And that's exactly why I was so surprised about this thing with Jade. Now I'd had her, I thought I'd have gotten her *out* of my system. Instead she was fucking with my head, even when she wasn't around.

I started feeling more sympathy for Cobra. I'd always teased him about his possessiveness with Mia: the way he wanted to own her, and went mental if another man just looked at her too long. And Mia was a beautiful woman, so it happened a lot. Especially when she had that glow about her when she was pregnant; then, men had found her irresistible. So much so that Cobra considered locking her up at home when he wasn't around. Understanding was beginning to dawn on me about how a man could feel like that.

It also said a lot about our brotherhood that he trusted me to live alone in a house with Mia and his two kids. Not that he really had a fucking choice with all those bullets lodged in his body.

Cobra brought me out of my thoughts with a slap on the back. "Hey man, I'm talking to you."

"What?"

"I said: I've organized for a barbeque next Sunday—here at the compound. Brothers need a morale booster. We need to get our fucking shit together. Show those motherfuckers we ain't scared or broken."

I sucked in a breath. *Fuck.* That would be dangerous. But Cobra was right—we were acting like scared pussies. It was time to get back in the saddle.

"Are you up to it, brother?" I was concerned that Cobra was trying to do too much too soon.

"Yeah. Fuck this shit. A man's gotta do what he has to do. Besides, I already spoke to Mia about it. She agrees it will be good for building the club spirit back up. In typical woman fashion, she's already planning the food."

Mia was levelheaded. I trusted her judgment. If she thought Cobra was up to it—and she should know—I'd go along with it.

I nodded. I'd just put extra security on for the day. Be extra careful, 'cause I had a tingling down my spine, and that didn't bode well.

Lexi sauntered back behind the bar counter, not looking in my direction. She smiled sweetly at an agitated Razor, and flirted outrageously with the man. Razor's frown melted and he seemed to lap up the attention. Was she trying to make me jealous? I chuckled to myself. *Bitches.* When would a man ever understand them? At least Razor was happy and was benefitting, so I just watched their interaction with amusement.

It still niggled at my mind: I knew Lexi from somewhere. But where?

"Ready to head back to LA?" I finished my beer and banged the glass down on the counter, suddenly eager to get back to the city.

CHAPTER 13

JADE

I wasn't sure exactly how to dress for the occasion. I'd never been to a barbeque at a MC compound. Why I'd even accepted Mia's invitation was beyond me. Mia had told me Ryder was living between the house and the compound since Cobra had come out of hospital. I guessed it was because he wanted to give the family their own space, yet needed to check that they were safe. I also knew that Ryder would use any excuse to go for a ride on his beautiful Harley.

But it was all a new experience for me. I was going into unknown and scary-as-hell territory. Especially after I'd had such tainted ideas of what bikers were all about for so long.

In my gut, I knew the answer: I wanted to see Ryder in his natural habitat, so to speak. I'd only ever seen him in LA, far away from his normal environment. The fancy house in Beverly Hills was out of his comfort zone, and

I'd picked that up from day one. So now I wanted to see the place where he was comfortable to just be himself.

Besides, I was an adult now, I had to find out for myself what a group of bikers were all about and make up my own mind. That didn't mean I wasn't still freaking out. Especially if Harrison found out about my plan. I shuddered just thinking about his reaction.

It was hot. Summer was in full-swing, and California was humid and uncomfortable. I chose a pair of denim shorts that I hadn't worn in years and a white tank top. Usually I was self-conscious about showing off my bare legs, but I wanted to be comfortable and just a little bit sexy. At the last minute, I slipped a shirt on, and tied a knot at my belly.

Both Mom and Daddy were on the patio, reading the Sunday paper over a cup of coffee. I poured some orange juice into a glass and made small-talk for a few minutes before announcing that I was off to a friend's place for the day.

"*Girl* friend or *boy* friend?" Mom asked. The woman was shrewd.

I laughed. "I'm going to a barbeque with a girl friend and her family. I adore her kiddies. And—I'm hoping to make lots of new friends—girls *and* boys."

"Remember lots of sunscreen. You don't want to burn and be sore tomorrow," she warned.

"And drink lots of water, especially if you're having alcohol," Daddy added.

They were just acting like they always did—caring and somewhat overprotective—but God, today it grated on my nerves. I rolled my eyes and sighed. They had to stop treating me like a damn kid.

Kissing both their foreheads, I headed off for the day. If they really knew where I was going they'd probably try to ground me.

Pressing the button to let the top of my convertible down, I decided I was going to enjoy the wind in my hair and just live for today. I wasn't going to worry about what Harrison and my parents would think. I was determined to have an open mind.

I got to the house in Beverly Hills within fifteen minutes. Mia had already strapped the kiddies into their car seats, and Cobra leaned against the SUV. Mia hugged me and pulled me by the hand—I was finally going to meet Cobra face-to-face.

To say that I was apprehensive was an understatement. What if he didn't like me? And what if he turned out to be everything I expected from a biker? How would I handle that?

At first he appeared intimidating. He was over six feet of brawn and muscle, a full sleeve tattooed on both arms with a piercing in his eyebrow. He looked mean, dressed in all black and with a scowl on his face. His head was completely shaven and his square jaw was set as he appraised me, arms folded over his wide chest. I couldn't see his eyes; they were hidden behind sunglasses.

Scary biker.

"Baby, this is the lovely Jade." Mia turned to Cobra and smiled. What I saw next shocked the hell out of me. The big man pushed away from the SUV and the biggest, warmest smile spread across his face. He removed his sunglasses as he held out a hand.

"So you're the girl who's caused so much fuss." His smile spread to his eyes, chocolate brown, just like Mia's and the kids. He took my hand in his and shook it, squeezing just enough so that it was welcoming but not painful. Small creases ran from his eyes to his mouth as he grinned.

Mia swatted his arm, laughing. "Baby, don't make

her uncomfortable."

"So who's been talking about me? Ryder? Only he'd think I make a fuss." I frowned. What had Ryder said about me? Remembering my manners, I held out my hand. "I'm glad you're out of the hospital. Your family missed you," I said politely. *Phew, he isn't that scary after all.*

With the formalities out of the way, I shuffled in next to Jamie, kissing the little ones and enjoying their welcoming smiles. Jamie had a picture book in his hands and was eager for me to read him a story. Well, at least if everything else tanked and I really didn't fit in, I could take the kids off Mia's hands and let her relax with her friends. Either way, it would work out.

As we got closer to the compound, I started doubting my decisions. Firstly, the decision to accept Mia's invitation. Curiosity had gotten the better of me, but I knew I wouldn't fit in, so it would be damn awkward. I came from a world so different, I didn't really have a clue what to expect.

Secondly, about what I was wearing. *Shorts, Jade? What the hell was I thinking?* There were going to be lots of guys around. I didn't want anyone to get the wrong impression. I should've worn jeans or a dress. But right now there was nothing I could do about it. *Suck it up, Princess.* I had to chuckle quietly to myself at the situation I'd found myself in. Who was I bluffing? I wanted Ryder's eyes to fall out when he saw me. I wanted him panting for me. Yes, I wanted his eyes, his hands and his mouth all over me . . .

I was conflicted between what I knew I *shouldn't* be doing, and what I wanted. My lust for Ryder was overwhelming, and making me do things that the old Jade would have slapped me for.

CHAPTER 14

JADE

My eyes widened when we reached the compound. Even the area looked different to what I was used to. It was industrial, and pretty desolated because it was a Sunday. Barbed wire rimmed the walls, and security guards stood at the imposing gates. Shit. What was the deal? Was this a mistake coming here? If they needed all these security measures . . .

Surely Mia wouldn't endanger the lives of her kids? That thought at least helped to settle the churning in my gut. My heart was hammering in my chest and my palms were clammy. Ryder wasn't expecting me. What would his reaction be when he saw me here—on his turf? Would he be mad? Well, I was going to find out soon enough.

The last time I'd seen Ryder was the night he'd broken into our house. I'd fallen asleep in his arms, at peace for the first time in years. And when I woke up in the morning, he was gone. He'd left the way he came. Silently. *Unexpectedly.*

I'd waited for Ryder to return every night since then, but he never came back. My heart ached, as if cold fingers gripped it and squeezed. The nightmares about *The Incident* were replaced by a fear that Ryder would completely avoid me now that he knew the whole story. He probably understood just how dangerous the situation was with Harrison, and had decided to move on.

That's what I wanted, right?

We'd arrived an hour before the party started because Mia wanted to set up a few things. She had organized for a few other wives and girlfriends—or 'old ladies', as I'd just learned bikers called their women—to help her, and of course, I'd help too.

The square in the middle of the buildings was barren except for a few benches. It was so different from the lush gardens I was used to. No wonder Ryder and particularly Mia wanted to rent the house in Beverly Hills because of the child-friendly garden for the kids.

A few other couples were setting up folding tables, chairs, and umbrellas. The men were carrying large buckets filled with ice and drinks. Everyone was chipping in to set up the party. Except for Ryder. I kept looking out for him, hoping to see him, but nothing.

Mia introduced me to the people already there. They were welcoming and friendly, completely *normal*. Why was I so worried I wouldn't fit in?

More and more people started arriving. I got really busy helping with the salads, and keeping an eye on the kids as Mia ran around ensuring there was enough meat and drinks to feed her extended family. Yet I kept listening for Ryder's voice. Disappointment washed over me. What if he didn't come to the barbeque? What if he was out with another woman? *Damn.*

Cobra introduced me to his brother, Razor. He looked just as mean and unyielding as Cobra initially had, especially wearing his cut and heavy biker-boots in spite of the weather. What was with that? Surely he didn't need to wear boots today? Around his forehead was a red bandana with skulls that made him look like a pirate. Yet, in spite of his appearance, Razor was really friendly, just like his brother. He was charming in an unaffected way.

"So, Jade, tell me about yourself. How did you become friends with Mia?" he asked as he helped me carry the bread rolls to the table.

I explained about the rental agency and how I'd sometimes babysit the kids, too. Razor laughed when I told him about the inspections I'd arranged because I'd believed there would be orgies and unsavory things happening at the house.

Razor had grabbed us each a cold beer, and we clinked the bottlenecks against one another. "Cheers, beautiful. You sure brighten up this place." He grinned appreciatively while his gaze raked up my body.

Smiling, I was just about to thank him for the compliment when I felt strong arms fold around my body and draw me back against a hard chest. *Ryder*. I'd recognize his smell anywhere. And the tingle that went down my spine before I even saw his face meant my body remembered the feel of him, too.

"Back the fuck off my woman, Razor. This one's taken," he growled.

Razor's eyes widened a fraction. "Hey, brother. How the fuck was I supposed to know that?" He held up both hands and laughed. "You never claimed a bit . . . woman before. Trust you to take the beautiful one."

"Ryder," I murmured, my breath hitching. *His woman?*

"She's all mine. And don't you forget that—at any time. I don't want to have to kill you, brother." He chuckled, but there was a seriousness to his tone that Razor couldn't ignore.

"Well, then, why weren't you here when she arrived?" Razor challenged.

Ryder pushed my hair aside and kissed my neck. It was such a possessive gesture, and I was taken by surprise.

"Maybe because Princess didn't tell me she was coming? Maybe because I was surprised as fuck to see her here. Wearing killer shorts that's sure to have every dick around here hard." His hand disappeared under my shirt and he stroked the soft flesh of my belly.

God. His warm breath on my neck... his possessive kiss... his hand stroking me... his husky voice. I could jump him right here, and not give a damn who watched. Instead, I giggled nervously. Like a damn teenager. A *horny* teenager, waiting to get laid. My pussy clenched as he turned me around to stare into my eyes.

"Hello Ryder," I breathed, feeling his erection press into my stomach. God, my need for him was growing by the second. My panties were soaked.

His eyes burned into mine. "Want to tell me how come you're here and I didn't know about it?" His voice was demanding, harsh even.

"Here you are. I was wondering where you were?" Mia walked over and slapped Ryder on the ass, like a big sister would. "I invited Jade. She's here as my guest. So everybody play nice, OK?" She eyed Razor who had a look of astonished amusement on his face.

Razor laughed. "Sure, Sister. Well, I for one am glad Ryder has his own woman. That means he won't be going after the one I want. Meaning that I won't have to kill him."

I'd nearly forgotten that Mia was married to Razor's brother. It was sweet how he called her 'sister'—I'd never have expected that from him. And now I was curious to know who the woman was that Razor fancied.

Mia squinted at Razor. "Wow, I'm gone for a few months and now you have your eye on somebody, too? Has Cupid been around lately, shooting a few stray arrows?"

Ryder rubbed my back, small circles caressing up and down my spine. I could hardly focus on the conversation. He was sending a clear message to every guy here that I was his. I couldn't have been more delighted that he wasn't afraid to claim me in front of everyone.

He dipped his head and whispered in my ear, his voice ominous. "I'm going to deal with you in a minute, Princess." His warm breath left a trail of goosebumps on my skin. I wasn't sure if I should be scared or happy. What I did feel, though, was a surge of energy rushing from my gut to my core, depositing more dampness onto my panties. Even my nipples tingled.

"Wet for me already, baby?" he whispered into my ear while squeezing my ass.

Sweet baby Jesus. *I may just orgasm right here in front of everyone.* I closed my eyes and pressed my thighs together. I was becoming a wanton slut. *Ryder's slut.*

My eyes flew open when I heard a woman's voice screeching.

"*She's* Princess? Fuck me!"

I looked straight into cousin Lexi's shocked eyes.

"Lexi? What the hell?" I gasped.

"Jade. What the fuck are you doing here? With Ryder practically dry humping you in front of everyone. Jesus, fuck. I didn't even know you knew him." Lexi was pissed off. Big time.

My cousin was a spitfire. She wasn't shy to say what she thought. I'd always had the opinion that she was a bit too outspoken, but she never cared what anyone thought of her. She'd always been a rebel, and Uncle Eric had his hands full raising her without a mother.

"I could ask the same question, cousin. The black hair? The tattoos and piercings? You look like a grunged-up biker girl. So different to when I last saw you at Christmas."

Ryder drew in a breath. He let go of me and took a step backward, staring—first at me, then at Lexi, then back again—as if we had just landed from an alien planet.

His shoulders shook with laughter. "Well, fuck me running. I'll be damned. So that's why you looked so familiar, Sheila. You're Jade's cousin!"

We both turned to him, glaring, hands on hips. Why in hell was Ryder calling my cousin *Sheila*? Had I missed something?

My eyes narrowed as I looked at first Lexi, then at Ryder. *Was Ryder fucking Lexi?*

Oh. My. God.

Please. No. *Just no.*

Other women—ones I didn't know—I may have been able to handle. *But my own cousin*? I felt my stomach drop.

"I work here. At the bar," Lexi said as she shook a cigarette from a packet and lit it, inhaling deeply. *She smoked?* What else didn't I—and Uncle Eric—know about Lexi?

"Lexi. You came." Razor was grinning like an idiot.

Was Razor sweet on Lexi? Was she the girl he referred to?

Jesus. My head was spinning. What the hell was going on?

CHAPTER 15

JADE

I swallowed hard. I had to know. I turned to Ryder. If he was fucking me and Lexi at the same time I just couldn't handle it.

I opened my mouth to speak, but before I could utter a word, Ryder growled. "Princess. My room. Now."

He grabbed my arm and led me inside the building. I felt everyone's eyes on my back as I followed Ryder, too stunned to speak. That didn't happen often.

Neither of us said a word. He marched us through the old building, past a bar filled with poker and pool tables. Past a huge kitchen where women were chattering as they dished food into large bowls. Past a large sitting room with a big-screen TV. Until we came to a door that he quickly unlocked.

I glanced at him from under my lashes. His jaw was set and his eyes blazing.

"Listen, Ryder—" I started.

He pushed me inside the room and locked the door. Seconds later I was up against the wall, Ryder's mouth stealing my breath. He kissed me hard, holding both my wrists in one large hand above my head, squeezing my breast with the palm of the other while jamming his knee against my sex to keep me still.

"Baby. What you do to me . . . and my cock. Fuck," he hissed.

"Ryder. Wait." *I need answers.*

"Why? I know you're here for me. To be fucked. And I want to. It's already been too long."

"Lexi," I panted, turning my head so he couldn't access my mouth. "Are you fucking Lexi?" I spat out.

Keeping my wrists pinned to the wall, he gripped my chin in his hand, squeezing my cheeks and turning my face till our eyes met.

"If I have, what's it to you?" he demanded, his voice hard.

I stared into his eyes, trying to read them, but all I could see was lust and arousal, his pupils were that dilated.

"If you are, I can't . . . I won't . . ."

"Why not?" he growled, his gaze searching my face.

"Because . . . because I want you to be only mine." I sensed with Ryder there was only one way. Brutal honesty.

"Fuck, Princess. *Fuck.*" He sucked my bottom lip into his mouth and bit into it.

I whimpered, oscillating between feeling pleasure and pain.

"What?" I murmured against his mouth. He hadn't answered my question yet.

"That's exactly what I want to hear." He kissed me till I was breathless, squeezing my breast hard so that ripples of longing traveled from my nipples to my pussy.

"Those fucking long legs of yours, I want them around my waist."

He undid the button of my shorts and pushed them down my legs, taking my panties down at the same time. Then he lifted me, pressing my naked ass against the wall.

"Undo me," he commanded in a husky voice.

My fingers fumbled at his jeans and he cursed because I was taking too long. My hair kept falling in front of my face. He gripped the strands in one hand, resting me on his knee till I freed his cock. Hissing through his teeth, he said two words: "Condom. Pocket."

I found the condom and ripped the foil between my teeth. I was becoming an expert at this. I rolled it on as he nibbled on my neck. God, my fingers were trembling and his lips on my neck were driving me wild.

"*Ahhh, baby*," he hissed as he thrust his cock into me, hard. His hand at the back of my head pulled my hair, opening my neck to him, and also preventing my head from hitting the wall as he rammed into me again and again, sucking and biting along my jawline at the same time.

"Fuck. I need you, Jade. Only you, baby. No other bitch."

Yes. I guess I got my answer. That was exactly what I'd wanted to hear. My heart swelled in my chest. With my legs wrapped tightly around his hips, Ryder drove into me, again and again, banging me so hard against the wall that I'd have concussion if his hand hadn't protected my head.

"Hold on," he groaned as he started coming inside me.

Turning around, he laid me on the bed, pulling out and disposing of the condom.

"That feels better. Now, Princess, I need to take care

of a few things."

"What's that?" I asked, my eyes wide. I had no idea what he meant. He hadn't let me come; I was still throbbing with need.

He sat on the bed and pulled me into his lap. Before I could cuddle into him, he flipped me around so that I was ass up. *Huh?*

He caressed my ass cheeks with large circular motions. His voice was soft, yet commanding. "I'm going to spank this beautiful fucking ass of yours. One: for questioning me about Lexi. Two: for wearing these fuck-me shorts. Three: for coming on to Razor when you thought I wasn't here. And four: for not telling me you'd be here. You will take these like the slut you are, then I will take care of your pussy."

Next thing, his hand rained down on my ass, spanking the shit out of me. He never hit the same spot twice, and each time his hand connected with my flesh, it sent ripples of pain and pleasure to my core. He'd caress my ass with feather-like strokes between each contact. Sweet Jesus, I never knew getting a spanking could make me even wetter. It was borderline painful, yet it turned me on beyond anything I'd ever imagined.

I bit into my bottom lip, tasting blood as I dug in hard, my hands gripping the bedcovers and twisting them in an attempt not to shout out. The last thing I needed was for the club members to come and investigate. Especially Mia or Lexi.

After the fourth hit, his fingers trailed lower, caressing over my wetness, then plunged inside me. This time I whimpered loudly, unable to stifle my pleasure any longer as he slowly finger-fucked me into ecstasy.

Shifting my weight off his lap, he knelt behind me, my ass still in the air, and admired the red welts that had formed on my ass, hissing between his teeth before lavishing the burning skin with his tongue. His mouth lowered, lapping my juices, circling my clit.

"Ryder," I gasped as my body trembled and spiraled into an orgasm. His tongue made its way inside me, fucking me as I rode my orgasm, his actions keeping it going for the longest time. I never knew I could orgasm this hard or this long. I had a lot to learn, and Ryder was teaching me just how much pleasure he could elicit from my body.

"Fuck, babe, I love when you say my name when you come. Yeah," he groaned.

He lay on the bed and pulled me into his arms, stroking my back and ass softly. I lay my head on his chest, listening to his erratic heartbeat, smiling as I realized that I was the one doing this to him.

"Babe, we need to talk about something."

"What is it, Ryder?" It was kind of weird lying in his arms, talking, and wearing only my top, naked from the waist down. I threw my leg over his in an attempt to hide my bare pussy.

He groaned. "Fuck. You want me riding you again? Rubbing your pussy against my leg is going to get you fucked. But I want it bare this time."

Ryder stayed silent for a minute, letting the weight of what he'd just implied sink in.

"You do?" I murmured, not sure exactly what to make of it.

"I want only you, Jade. And I don't want you fucking anyone else, either. I want us to be exclusive. You're mine now, babe, and I want to feel you, skin to skin. That OK with you?"

I reached up and stroked his cheek. Here was my big badass biker, so fucking alpha in every way, telling me how, when, and where he was going to fuck me, asking if I was OK. Feelings of warmth surged through my heart. I couldn't be happier than in this moment.

I pulled his face down so that he was looking into my eyes. I wanted to see him when we discussed this. "I'm all safe. I'm on the pill. Went on when I started dating Marcus."

A feral growl escaped his lips when I mentioned Marcus. Guess it was still a sore point. I loved that Ryder was so possessive and so . . . primal. The very things I'd hated about him before were now the things I loved about him. OK, maybe *love* was too strong a word. But it felt right. Yes, I was feeling more for Ryder than just lust; I was falling in love. Hard. To the point that I wanted nothing more than to be with Ryder 24/7. Talking, cuddling, doing everyday things . . . and, of course, wild passionate fucking, too. *Lots of that.*

"How many men have you . . . been with?" His breath hitched.

"If I answer that question, you have to be prepared to do the same. Are you?"

He stayed quiet for a long time. I waited for him to say something. Just as I was about to give up on him replying, he answered.

"Jade, I'm not going to lie to you. I've had plenty of bitches over the years. More than I care to count. But they were nothing to me. Bodies to satisfy my needs and urges. Faceless fucks."

I drew in a sharp breath. I was so inexperienced compared to him. I was amazed he even wanted someone like me.

"Baby, it's been pure hell trying to stay away from you. Since the other night, when you told me your story, I've done a lot of soul searching. I've been outside your house every evening, dying to come inside to be with you. But I had to give you time, too. And today you came to me. It means you can't stay away either, in spite of what you say."

It was true. Even if the flame of desire burned me to death, I couldn't stay away or stop myself wanting him.

He gripped my chin in his hand and gazed into my eyes, as if he were searching deep into my soul. He spoke softly, reverently. "I never knew someone like you existed. I never knew I could feel like this about another person. I can't name what I feel, because I've never felt it before.

"All I can do is to tell you how happy it makes me feel when I'm near you. And how fucking amazing it feels when I'm inside you. I think of you from the moment I open my eyes till the moment I close them. There's not a minute of a day I'm not thinking of you, aching for you, wanting to be inside you. *Only you, babe; nobody else.* If you can name that, then you know how I feel about you."

I sucked in a breath. He was describing exactly how I felt about him. I'd also never felt like this before. I didn't have a name for it, either. I let go of my bottom lip that I'd been biting down on. "I think we are more than in lust with one another," I said, searching for the right words, "I think we are . . . we are *obsessed* . . . with one another," I whispered.

He laughed softly. "Yeah, I sure am. I want you to be mine, and only mine."

My finger traced his stubbled jaw. I smiled at him. "I want that too. To be only yours, Ryder."

Both hands cupped my face as he kissed me hard, possessively, hungrily. I unashamedly rubbed my naked pussy against his leg till he groaned into my mouth. His cock, which had been half-mast, resting on his stomach, was nudging my hip. He pulled me on top of his chest and I slid down, taking him bare.

His eyes rolled back in his head. "Jesus. Christ. Fuck."

"Like it, baby?" I whispered near his ear.

"Hell yeah. You feel so good, babe."

My heart swelled at his words. I loved that I could do this to him. Yet I was getting deeper into trouble. For a moment, my thoughts drifted to my family. What the hell was I going to do about them and in particular about Harrison? The problem was getting bigger every time I let Ryder fuck me. He thrust into me again, and his action pulled me back into the present.

At this moment I wanted nothing more than to be right here, with Ryder, his cock deep inside me, stretching me, filling me to capacity, so that my mind and body was only his. I didn't want to think about anything else. Just us.

He kissed me, long and hard, taking my breath away before he rolled us over. This time I was underneath him, his arms on both sides of my face. He stared into my eyes. "Want to see your beautiful eyes when you come, baby," he ground out as he thrust rhythmically into me. It was the first time he was slow and gentle.

"Want to fucking see into your heart and your soul."

Sweet Lord. Since when was my badass biker so deep and caring?

He completely undid me.

Killing me with his words.

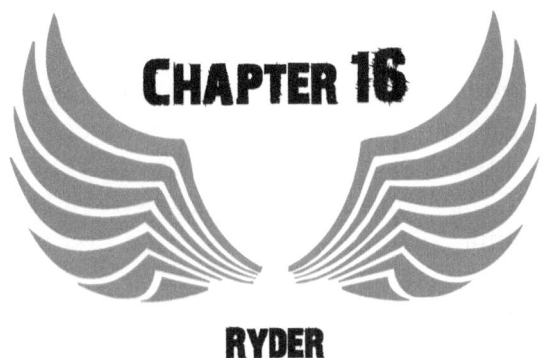

CHAPTER 16

RYDER

Fuck. It was hard to keep my eyes off her ass. The way she leaned over the pool table was designed to make me so hard that I lost all concentration on the game. Whoever said that women didn't know what they were doing when they challenged men to a game of pool hadn't seen Jade and Lexi work the room.

The two cousins had a talk in the bathroom; the place women always disappeared to in pairs or groups. Someday I wanted to be a fly on the fucking wall, and just see for myself what the hell chicks got up to in there. Anyway, they went in rather annoyed with one another and came out twenty-five minutes later, looking hot as hell and laughing as if nothing had happened before they'd disappeared into that mysterious place.

Jade and I had been in my room for well over an hour, and if I had my way, we'd never have left the bed. But it was Cobra's homecoming barbeque, and I had to be respectful of my pres and be part of it. Besides, all that fucking made me hungry, and I knew the women would've gone all out to put on a good spread.

So after kissing the shit out of Jade, I eventually let her leave the room so we could go find food. Now that she'd agreed to be only mine, I was a happy man.

We decided to get out of the heat and play a few games of pool. It started as a joke—the cousins had challenged Razor and I to a game. We'd winked at one another, thinking we'd let them win the first few games before beating them. It turned out these girls were a formidable team. I could see the other guys were impressed as fuck.

"Are you boys a little afraid we're going to clean up the table?" Lexi asked, quirking an eyebrow at Razor, who was so cunt-struck he was just the worst partner I'd ever had. I sighed. What a pathetic pair we made.

Ratbag answered before anyone else. "Never. Ain't no Sheilas ever beat Ryder and Razor."

"Well, then, watch history being made tonight," Jade said, with a sweet butter-won't-melt-in-my-mouth kind of smile, as she sank the next ball into the pocket. I whistled beneath my breath. Princess had mad skills. Looking at her, I'd assume she wouldn't have a fucking clue how to even hold a cue, never mind play like a fucking pro. Her and Lexi were winning and not just because they were using their sexual charms, but because they actually really knew how to play the goddamn game.

Jade leaned over the table, and in those shorts, her legs seemed to go on forever. And fuck me, if every guy in the room wasn't salivating as they gawked at her, probably fantasizing about being between those sexy pins. *Note to self: Forbid Jade to wear shorts to the compound again.* Fuck, Hammer and Ratbag were perving so hard on my woman, I wanted to fucking punch them. I gave them a warning glare to back off, which they understood and grinned sheepishly at being caught in the act.

Finally, it was my turn to play. The balls had been set up in such a way that I had to concentrate really hard to get the angle right, but I was determined to sink this number nine. Just as I was about to hit the ball, Jade leaned over to pick up the chalk she had 'accidentally' dropped, teasing me with her perfect tits. Her eyes locked with mine for a split second, and fuck, I missed.

Razor smirked. "Ryder. Fuck, man, you could do that move in your sleep. Stop staring at your bitch and play the fucking game."

We should have quit while we were ahead. Each game, we doubled the bets. Each game, we got further behind. By now, half of the club was inside the bar, howling with laughter that Razor and I were getting our asses kicked by two women.

Razor and I were just about to win our first game when Ox came storming in to the clubhouse. Hi expression was murderous. His face was flushed, and thick veins were popping on his forehead. Was he furious about Razor and Lexi? When Ox was angry, anybody who valued their life thought twice before they challenged him—it would be a seriously dumb mistake.

"Ox? What's up, brother?" I wanted to diffuse any problems before it got ugly. Today was not the day for fights about pussy.

"Fucking cops at the gate. They have a search warrant. And one of them is acting like a raving lunatic, threatening to kill me if I don't open the fucking gates."

Cobra was the first to react.

"Jesus. *Fuck*. Can't they just leave us alone for one day? I'll go talk to them."

Mia stepped in front of Cobra. "No honey, please. You're not . . . ah, God . . . please let somebody else handle this?" Her voice was filled with panic. I couldn't blame her after what they'd been through.

I put an arm on Cobra's shoulder in an attempt to settle him down. "Hey, time I stepped up to the VP challenge. Let me talk to the fuckers. OK?"

He was still staring at Mia's face when he nodded. Guess she got to him.

"We're coming with ya." Razor, Hammer and Ox fell in behind me as I turned to leave.

I stopped Ratbag from following. "Look after the Sheilas, bro," I ordered. "Keep them safe."

Ratbag swallowed hard. Realizing that he'd been given the most important job of all, he nodded his head. A deep frown marred his brow. I guessed that the enormity of the responsibility was sinking in, yet I knew I could trust Ratbag to do as asked.

Marching to the gate, I was mad as hell. We were having a family barbeque, for fuck's sake. Why did the fuckers think they needed to come and ruin the party? It was sunset, and we'd had a peaceful day so far, everyone enjoying the day, being together as one big happy family. Until this intrusion. *Fuck.*

The big motherfucker with his hands on the gate, his knuckles white because he was gripping so tightly, caught my eye first. He was a brute of a man, and I was used to big guys like Ox.

He wasn't dressed in uniform. Instead he wore black jeans and a black T-shirt. A beanie covered his head and his jaw was set in stone as he glared at me, hatred burning in his eyes. As I drew closer, I noticed the tattoo on the inside of his muscled forearm. Underneath the scales of justice were the words: "Justice for all."

Angry cop. Fuck.

"Open this gate. Now," he commanded, a sneer on his face as he held up his badge.

I sucked in a breath when I read his name. Very fucking angry cop. Harrison fucking Summers. *Jade's brother.*

Shit just got real.

CHAPTER 17

RYDER

I couldn't signal to Ratbag to hide Jade and Lexi in the safe place. Jesus, why hadn't I thought of that before coming out? I should've guessed it was a matter of time before her brother came to the compound to snoop.

Did he know that Jade and Lexi were here?

Hammer caught my eye, and by the frown on his face I knew he'd worked out that this was connected to Jade. He'd helped me look up information on Jade and her cop brother online after Jade had told me the story about the incident, so he'd recognize his name.

I nodded ever so slightly. Hammer was the smart one, like my brother, Max, who was usually two steps ahead of everyone else. He turned on his heels and walked slowly back to the clubhouse. I knew it took every inch of control for him not to run. But if he did, it would raise alarm bells. Acting as if he was just bored was far smarter. But inside, my guts were churning.

Hurry the fuck up, Hammer. *Get Jade and Lexi to the safe place.* I was struggling to keep my exterior cool and relaxed. As if this was nothing unusual. I had to buy time.

"So, what do you want to see?" I baited.

"Just open the fucking gates, asshole. We'll talk inside," he growled, even baring his teeth as a feral animal would to show his intent of ripping anything that stood in his way apart.

Ox groaned behind me. He was struggling to remain calm. I knew he was just dying to lay into the angry cop. If I weren't careful, we'd have a fucking fistfight on our hands. Well, maybe that *wasn't* such a bad idea . . . Only problem was, we were outnumbered three to one and besides, that would just alert them into thinking we had something to hide, and make them even more determined to snoop around the compound.

"Yeah? I don't give a fuck what kinda badge you wearing. If you're on my territory, you don't talk to me like that without getting your fucking nose broken." I squinted and stared him down. Harrison's hand went to his nose instinctively. That's when I noticed it was already screwed. He must've had it broken before.

Jesus. A cop with a death wish. There was nothing worse. They were the kind of vigilantes that took the law into their own hands—shooting first, and questioning after. I had to stay calm for Jade's sake. As much as I wanted to punch the fucker in the face and make his nose bleed, I had to rein it in.

Harrison shook the bars in front of him. "I'm counting to three. If you don't open the fucking gate, we are shooting it open." As if that was a signal, the uniformed cops lifted their guns. Jesus, Harrison wasn't playing a game of chicken. He had balls of fucking steel. I had to admire that about a man, even if he was on the other team.

I nodded to Razor. He knew the drill. Pretending to be so nervous that he forgot the code and kept punching in the wrong numbers. Razor hated playing scared, because he was a really mean motherfucker. Ever since he and Cobra saved me all those years ago, I'd never seen Razor scared of anything.

Harrison saw straight through the ruse. "Quit stalling," he barked at Razor. Razor rolled his eyes back in his head, clenching his jaw as he aggressively punched in the right numbers. Fuck, Razor wanted to go to town on the cops. He was even wearing his custom shoes with the razorblades imbedded into the soles. We'd have a fucking bloodbath on our hands.

"Razor, chill," I reminded him. That was the great thing about being brothers. We only needed a word to convey a whole message. Razor shook his head, like a wet dog would, as if ridding himself of his thoughts. He had just as much at stake here, even though he wasn't aware that Harrison Summers was related to the girl he was sweet on. I hadn't told him that part yet. Fuck, I hadn't known before earlier today that he was soft on that bitch.

Why the fuck was Harrison Summers here?

Was it coincidence, or did he know his sister and cousin were here? I just hoped that none of the brothers or their bitches would say anything out of place. None of them were aware of this situation. Not even Cobra or Mia. *Fuck.*

Once the gates opened, Harrison strode forward, pushing Razor out of the way with one hand. Fucker was strong. Razor growled, ready to retaliate, but I shook my head, showing him to back off—for now, at least.

"*Where is she?*" Harrison growled, indicating with a

nod toward the clubhouse. The cops immediately raised their weapons and stalked the clubhouse.

I held up my hands. "She? Who are you talking about?" Jesus, he was here as Jade's brother, here to protect her. *But she was my woman. I wanted to protect her, too.* This was all kinds of fucked up.

"Jade. My little sister. I'm taking her home with me."

My mouth went dry. Fuck, he'd just commanded up ten fucking cops and a search warrant to help him fetch his sister? He didn't mess around. He meant fucking business.

"And Lexi, my cousin. I know she works here. Well tonight, that changes."

I gripped Razor's t-shirt and fisted it tightly, holding him back. I wasn't sure how much longer I'd be able to keep everything under control. Praying that Hammer had gotten Jade and Lexi to the safe place, I watched the cops burst into the clubhouse. Only a few steps behind, I wanted to see if the girls were gone.

The boys were playing pool, some hanging by the bar, others around the dartboard, as if nothing unusual was happening. A few women were chatting away on the couches, holding their kids on their laps.

Thank fuck. All those drills in the past had paid off. Everyone was acting as if this was just any Sunday night at the clubhouse. I swallowed hard. Fuck, I loved these people.

Harrison nodded toward the rooms. "Open every door. We won't rest till we find the girls. I know they're here. The sooner they come out, the better for everyone. I'll tear this place to fucking pieces if I have to."

I believed him. Rage was radiating in waves from every pore in his body.

I just hoped that Ratbag got it right.

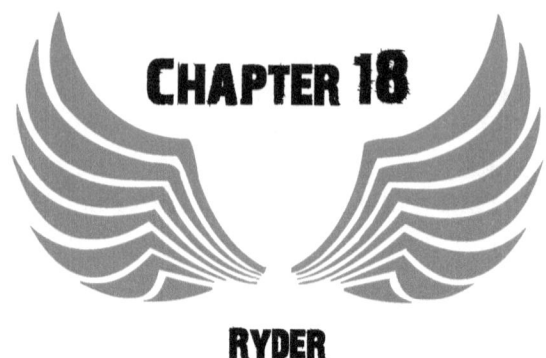

CHAPTER 18

RYDER

My heart nearly jumped out of my chest.

"Hello, cousin. Fancy seeing you here." Lexi's sultry voice behind me sent goosebumps scattering across my skin. Jesus fucking Christ. Why was she still here?

"Lexi," Harrison growled, "Where's Jade? Is she still in the bathroom?" His gaze went to the door from which Lexi had just emerged.

"Nah, she went home ages ago. Jade and me had a huge fight. As usual. She stormed out of here, saying she'd never go anywhere with me again. Sorry," she looked at him from under her lashes, all apologetically, as if she knew she'd done wrong.

"Jade's left? How come I didn't know that? This place is under surveillance 24/7." Smirking, he grinned at me. "Yeah, just in case you didn't know," he said, a clear warning in his tone.

"Yeah, I convinced her to come to the barbeque

with me. You know, after what happened with Marcus, I thought she should get out a bit. So I dragged her here. Then we had a fight, and she went home. Probably sulking in her room now."

Harrison dialed a number on his phone. Smart fucker. My hands were clammy as I fisted them by my sides, my heart racing, pumping adrenaline through my body.

"Jade? Where the fuck are you?" he barked down the phone.

I watched the expression on his face soften as he heard her voice. Yes, I wanted to know too. Where the fuck was Jade? Ratbag was nowhere to be seen.

Harrison closed his phone and instructed his second-in-charge to call back his troops.

One of the women piped up. "Oh yeah, Ratbag took Jade home ages ago. She said she had a stomachache."

I swallowed hard. Ratbag must've taken her out the secret back way. While I was relieved that she was safe and that we'd avoided a bloodbath here tonight, I didn't want her at home and so far away from me.

"Lexi, you're coming home with me. Get your stuff. Let's go."

"OK. But only because I was ready to go anyway. I got a bit too much sun today, and I'm tired. But Harrison?"

He cocked his head. "Yeah?"

"I'm a grown woman. And I work here. It's my job to be here. This is how I earn my rent. You have to respect that. OK?"

"Find another job, Lexi. You aren't coming back here, sweetheart." He turned to me. "Consider this Lexi's resignation. She just quit her fucking bar job."

Harrison placed his gun back into its holster and took her by the arm. "Jade's in her room, reading, as you predicted. I'll have a talk with her tomorrow about coming here. Neither you nor Jade will put a foot in this place again. Are we clear, little cousin?"

Lexi nodded. "Let me just get my stuff," she said as she wriggled free of Harrison's hand on her and went behind the bar to get her purse.

I saw Razor go after her. I had to distract Harrison.

"You said your sister is safely at home?" I quirked an eyebrow, keeping my voice as neutral as possible.

"Yeah. And she's never coming here again. Of that, I will make one hundred percent certain."

Watching the last of the cops filter out of the clubhouse, I smirked. "Well, you guys can stop snooping and watching us. We can take care of our own."

"Yeah? Like the raid by the LA Demons? Getting him shot?" He nodded his head toward Cobra. "You think you're safe? I've got news for you. You delve into criminal activities, you're never safe. I'll give my last breath to ensure that. Consider this a friendly warning. Next time I come here, I will rip this fucking place apart. Got that?"

My fists balled by my sides. *Self-righteous prick.* "I hope our paths don't cross again anytime soon. I don't know if I can reel it in enough not to punch your smug face and make you bleed," I retorted. *Fuck this shit.*

Why the hell did Jade have to have a brother who was a fucking cop? Especially one out for vengeance? But that wasn't going to stop me.

No, it only made me more determined to fight for her. Our worlds may have been colliding, but I knew what I wanted: Jade.

I wasn't letting anything tear us apart. None of this bullshit was going to stand in my way because I had no other choice—Jade was the woman for me. I knew that now.

I didn't want to be in this world if it was without her.

So bring it on. I was ready to fight for my Princess till my last breath.

Fuck, yeah.

CHAPTER 19

JADE

"Sis. Would your planning to move out have anything to do with the Scorpio Stinger MC? And in particular a man named Ryder Knox?"

I sucked in a breath. *Jesus.* How did he know?

"Where did you get that idea?" I was trying to buy time. I had to find out how much my brother knew before I gave him an answer. Maybe he was just guessing. Growing up in a house with an attorney for a father and a cop for a brother had schooled me well in the art of interrogation. And now that I was a qualified lawyer myself, I used those tricks to my own advantage. *Always answer a question with a question.* It worked every time.

"I have my informants. Plus, I know you've been on the back of his bike. Dad told me about the night with Marcus. I must say, as much as I hate bikers, I kind of owe him one for saving you from that scumbag."

Harrison's jaw and fists were clenched tightly. His protective instincts were in high gear. I had to use this to my advantage.

"Yeah, can you believe what Marcus did? So when Ryder appeared out of nowhere, it was like my savior arrived on a shiny metal horse. At the time, it was the best option." I shrugged, trying to play it down. I didn't want Harrison sniffing around Ryder.

"OK, I get that. But you should've taken a taxi straight home. Not gone off for the night with a biker boy. After The Incident, I didn't think you'd ever do such a thing, Jade." His voice was stern, and a deep frown furrowed his brow. I hated seeing him so glum.

"Harrison, that was a long time ago. We have to let go of those bad memories and move on with our lives. We can't let what happened ten years ago still cloud our lives and our future."

He groaned as he sank back in the chair and closed his eyes. I knew his pain was still there, but he had to let the scab grow over it so that it could finally heal. Keeping the wound raw only meant it would never get any better.

I placed my hand on his arm, stroking gently. "The bikers who killed Amy and the others were all apprehended and served their sentences. They have done their time. But you, living like this—*you're* the one still serving time."

His eyes flew open and he sat forward, grabbing my wrist and twisting till it hurt.

"Don't say that, Sis. I can't ever let it go. That would mean I've let Amy and her memory down." He paused for a beat, clearly lost in his thoughts. Raw pain flickered in his eyes. He swallowed hard before he continued, his voice sadder than I'd heard it in a long time. "I never told you this, because you were too young: Amy was seven weeks pregnant. We were going to tell our parents a week later. I was going to *marry* her."

"Oh God, Harrison, why haven't you ever told me before? Now I understand your pain so much better. Her death was a terrible thing. But the baby—" I slapped my hand over my mouth. Finally I was getting why Harrison carried so much hatred toward bikers and MC clubs, and refused to let it go.

His shoulders slumped as he leaned forward, his head in his hands. "All of that was taken from me. By bikers with illegal guns. *I can never let that go.* I will hunt fuckers like them down, and stop that from happening to anyone else," he ranted, his pain in his eyes.

"That's noble of you, Harrison. I get where you're coming from. But Amy—she would never have wanted you to suffer this much and for this long. She'd want you to be happy—even without her. That's how much she loved you."

He ran a hand through his hair, despair evident on his face. "There isn't a day that passes that I don't think about her, about what could've been... you're probably right in saying that Amy would've wanted me to move on, but it's not that simple."

I rubbed slowly up and down his arm. "You're not going to like what I'm going to say to you now. But just hear me out." I took a deep breath. Giving my older brother advice wasn't something I'd done before—especially about matters of the heart. But seeing him still hurting this badly, made my heart squeeze. "Maybe there is someone else out there for you. Someone who *can* bring you happiness."

Waiting with bated breath for his reaction, my heart pounded in my ears. Had I gone too far?

Harrison shook his head. "I doubt I can even allow myself to love again. It's just too painful. And if something ever happened to you, I don't think I'd be able to cope with that. That's why you have to promise me to stay away from the biker guy. It can't work out—you're from two completely different worlds. I don't want to see you get hurt, but even worse, if he so much as damages a hair on your head, I'll be after him. And it won't be pretty."

"You're my big brother, and you care about me—I get that. But you can't stop me from seeing who I want to. I'm a big girl now. If I want to see Ryder . . ."

"So you *are* seeing him then!" he barked.

Damn. I walked straight into that one. Harrison outwitted me after all by catching me off-guard. He grabbed my upper arms and shook me. "Jade. Have you forgotten what kind of people they are? That they kill innocent people? How could you?"

"It's not like that," I retorted, annoyed that he was jumping to conclusions before knowing the story. "I've known Ryder for a while now. Yes, his background is different to mine, but that doesn't make him a bad person. It merely means we are different in some ways. But we are both humans, with the same wants and desires. Besides, I'm not *dating* him, so calm down."

"Calm down? Shit, Jade, I've got news for you. Ryder Knox and his little gang are on my radar. The shooting that went down a few months ago? That was based on illegal guns being shipped around. The same kind of guns that killed Amy and my friends back then, and that still kill innocent people every day now. I will bring those motherfuckers down, even if it costs me my life."

I jumped up, my hands on my hips, and stared at my brother through narrowed eyes. "For a smart man, you're so damn stubborn. Like Ryder said, even the law gives him more credit than we do, by believing he is innocent till proven guilty," I huffed.

Harrison shook his head. "Fuck me. It's worse than I'd thought. What? You're quoting a biker now? Jesus, Jade, what's gotten into you? I think I need to hunt that fucker down and put an end to this shit before it gets out of hand. You're going nowhere near Biker Boy again. Are we clear? I'll arrest him, and throw his fucking ass into jail if you don't listen to me."

"On what grounds?"

"You don't realize I have a whole fucking file on the Scorpio Stinger MC and their rivals. I can dig up dirt and make it stick. And I will if you don't stay away. You have no fucking idea what you're getting into. These bikers are criminals. They deal in illegal guns, and drugs, and extortion." A vein ticked in his neck. His lips were drawn into a thin line as he stared at me through narrowed eyes. It's not pretty. And I won't allow you to be any part of that shit. Do. You. Understand?"

Blood rushed to my head and anger swirled in my gut. "Just because Ryder had a tough upbringing doesn't make him a goddamn *criminal*. You can't generalize like that."

Harrison's fists clenched and unclenched. The frown between his eyes deepened. "OK. I wasn't going to tell you this..." He closed his eyes for a few seconds. When he opened them, they were hard and calculating. "Ryder *killed* a man. His own father, no less, when he was only a kid of eleven." His voice had a hard edge I couldn't ignore. "That just smells like trouble. He was in juvie for years. That's how he got tangled up with the Scorpio Stinger MC. And now he's their VP. Come-on Sis, even you know what all of that means."

Harrison wouldn't lie to me.

All the blood drained from my face as I went cold.

"Yeah, I can see Ryder omitted to tell you about his childhood. Killing a man is a big deal. And he did it in cold blood, and had no remorse after. That makes him a psycho killer. *Dangerous.* Like fuck am I letting him anywhere near my little sister."

"Harrison!"

"Do you hear me Jade? Over my fucking dead body are you hooking up with a biker. I'll kill him with my bare hands if he touches you."

RYDER

For the first time since meeting Cobra that fateful day in juvenile detention, I wanted to kill him. I'd never have believed that this day would come. But it had. Cobra was staring me down, anger seething from his pores. In his neck, a thick vein protruded and throbbed, and a grim expression was on his face.

"Look, I'm mad as hell at Mia for inviting Jade in the first place. But Mia didn't know about the connection with her cop brother. But you, Ryder . . . *you* could have stopped it all from happening. I don't appreciate the fucking cops showing up at the compound. It could've turned nasty. For fuck's sake, we had old ladies and kids here." He closed his eyes for a minute.

When he opened them again, pain was etched across his face. "I have nothing against Jade as a person. But I can never allow the bloodshed and loss of our family again on my watch."

"I know, brother. This is on me, not you."

He scrubbed a big hand over his face. Cobra looked tired. All of this had taken a toll on him—the shootout, him nearly dying, Mia losing the baby, the cop raid last night. He looked older than his thirty-six years.

"I tossed and turned all night about this. And I've come to a decision. Neither Jade nor Lexi can ever come to the compound again. It's too fucking risky. And I'm all done with taking risks where my family's lives are involved."

The blood drained from my face. "What are you saying, Cobra?" I snarled. My gut turned upside down—I knew what was coming, and I didn't like it one bit.

"I'm saying that you should forget about that woman. I'll deal with Razor and Ox about Lexi. But now, I'm telling you—brother to brother—that you should walk away from Jade while you still can, and before it brings more shit to the club."

I shook my head. Had I heard right? Cobra was telling me in no uncertain terms to end it with Jade? Fuck.

"Cobra. You don't know what you are asking, man." Sweat formed on my brow, and I felt a trickle run down my back. Cobra didn't understand. *Give up Jade?* I was beyond that stage. The realization hit me with full force, making my knees so weak that I had to grip the ends of his desk to keep myself standing upright. My knuckles were white as I held on, my brain in a whirl.

"I'm fully aware of what I'm asking. I'm asking that you sacrifice pussy for the club. It's always been an easy decision for you, Ryder. A no-brainer. Why the resistance now?"

"Well—this time it's *different*. Because Jade isn't just pussy to me. She's *my* bitch. My woman. I fucking *love* her. Yeah." There: I'd finally declared it, to my boss and president no less. Finally, I was able to formulate all those crazy feelings into words.

Cobra's eyes widened and his skin went ashen. He slammed a fist on the table.

"Fuck. Why her, Ryder? Of all the fucking bitches in the world . . . It can't work, brother. You're from different worlds. She's the rich bitch, and you're the bad biker. Do I fucking need to remind you of that?"

"Christ, Cobra, do you think I chose this? Do you think I wanted to love the snarky bitch that pushes all my buttons—good and bad? No. I didn't choose it. *It chose me.* My fucking heart can't be told who to love and who not to love. It fucking is what it is, brother."

I sank into the chair, spearing my fingers through my hair. This was as fucked up as it could get. *Cobra telling me to let go of Jade.* Did he fucking know what he was asking of me?

I hung my head, letting it rest on my chest as I closed my eyes. Anything. I would do anything for Cobra, anything for my brothers and the Scorpio Stinger MC.

Anything, but this.

Because fuck me, now that I'd tasted the love of a woman as sweet as Jade, I wanted more of it. Cobra could *not* be asking me to give up this one thing I wanted more than my next breath.

Cobra cleared his throat. "As your president, I'm asking you, Ryder. I'm asking for all the lives of your brothers, past and present. Let Jade go. You know there can come no good of it. You know it's fucked. It will lead to bloodshed. *You know.*"

I jumped up from the chair. *Fuck.* I needed to punch something—anything. I slammed one fist into the wall, then another. It hurt like fuck, but it was nothing like the pain of my heart that was breaking in two. I'd waited all my life to feel like this. Since the day Marianne had left, and never come back. Since when first the emptiness, and then the hatred had filled my heart. And now that I'd finally found *my woman*, Cobra was forbidding it?

"Cobra. You're my brother. I love you as if you were my own flesh and blood. Because to me, you are. But what you're asking—it's impossible. Jade is a part of me I don't want to live without. She's what makes all the years of pain and torment worthwhile. Because I now understand that I had to go through all of that to get to her, so that I could understand what a special gift it is, to be given a love like that. And you, of all people, should know how it feels. Imagine me asking you to give up Mia."

He growled, shaking his head. He'd rather die than give up Mia. Surely he could understand how I felt? We were bikers, yes. We were criminals, yes. But we were also just human. We loved and hurt as deeply as everyone else. *Maybe even deeper.*

His mouth drew into a thin line. "Fuck. You are making it hard on us both. You know I love you as my own brother. I want to see you happy with your woman. But it can't be Jade. You have to understand this, Ryder. You and Jade together is bad news for her family and for us—*your family.* You're a modern-day fucking Romeo and Juliet. Yeah, I know about that shit, I'm a biker, not a dumbass." He smiled wryly as he paced the room. This was killing Cobra as much as it was killing me.

"Say goodbye to Jade. Let it be done. It will be better for everybody." *Everybody but me—and Jade.*

Our two worlds were colliding. We were being torn apart. *Fuck.* I couldn't let it happen.

Jade—and our love—was worth fighting for.

Does she believe that too? Fuck.

CHAPTER 21

JADE

Three nights after Harrison's surprise visit at the compound, I still hadn't heard from Ryder. Was all that talk of being his woman just crap he came up with to get me to have sex with him? Maybe he got off on dominating woman, telling them he owned them. Then when he tired of them, he moved on to the next target.

Fortunately, I had a really big case to work on at Summers, Walker and Hedgewick, so it kept me pretty occupied during the day. But at night, I lay in my bed, my mind ticking over, running the events nonstop through my brain, like a movie on repeat.

The sweet words Ryder had spoken to me were a refrain by now, I knew them by heart: *I never knew someone like you existed. I never knew I could feel like this about another person.* It brought a smile to my face, and lightness to my heart. His admission made my toes curl, simply because the same thing had happened to me too, but I wasn't going to ever admit it to him: *I think of you from the moment I open my eyes till the moment I close them. There's not a minute of a day I'm not thinking of you, aching for you, wanting to be inside you.* And my absolute favorite: *Only you, babe, nobody else.*

But now . . . where was he? I didn't want to believe that he scared this easily. Was what we were both feeling not worth exploring? It was new, it was strange, and it was scary as hell. But it felt really, really good.

What was this thing we both felt? Was it possible that it was...love? The expression on his face when he tried to explain how he felt made my heart beat a little faster. *I can't name what I feel, because I've never felt it before. All I can do is to tell you how happy it makes me feel when I'm near you. And how fucking amazing it feels when I'm inside you. If you can name that, then you know how I feel about you.*

A pang shot through my heart. I missed Ryder—his smell, his warmth, and the way he made me feel when he was close. I wanted to be around him every day. Somehow, my life felt empty when the larger-than-life man wasn't around.

My phone beeped beside me. Ryder? I glanced at the screen, hopeful. But no. It was my cousin from Australia. "Rebecca? How are you?" I asked. A chat with her would take my mind off my hassles.

"Jade. Sorry to call so late, honey. I'm planning to make a trip to LA in six weeks. Do you think we could catch up again?"

When I last met Rebecca in New York a few months ago, we'd had a fun time together. I needed a distraction. Plus, she was a smart woman and I valued her opinion; maybe I could ask her for advice.

"Of course we can. It'll be great to see you. I can show you around LA. In fact, come and stay with us?"

"Oh no, I'm coming for work. Usually my boss puts me up in style at a fancy hotel. But I'd love to go on a shopping trip and maybe have a girl's night out one evening?"

"OK. Sounds good. Let me know the dates and I'll set it all up. We'll have a blast."

"Jade, how's your relationship coming along? Are you engaged to Marcus yet? Are the wedding invitations coming any time soon?"

I rolled my eyes. Of course—the last time I saw Rebecca, Marcus was courting me. I'd forgotten that I hardly knew Ryder at the time. It felt so long ago.

"Marcus? Oh Lord no, we didn't get engaged. Long story. But he has asked me to accompany him to the annual partner's ball."

A growl from my bedroom door startled me. My head jerked up and my gaze fell on Ryder, leaning against the doorjamb, arms folded, a deep frown marring his brow.

"Rebecca, I've got to go, honey. Something came up. But we'll talk soon, okay?"

We said our goodbyes and I hung up, stunned that Ryder had snuck into the house again and was staring down at me, his eyes narrowed, and his jaw set in stone.

"No Marcus. Not happening. *Over my dead fucking body,*" he growled. "If you want him to stay alive, tell him to fuck off from my woman."

"Ryder," I breathed. Where had he appeared from so suddenly?

"Yeah, babe. I had to come see you."

"Doesn't your phone work? Why don't you call me?"

He smirked. "I am calling you. Live and in person. It's so much better than a damn phone call, don't you think?"

"And what about the other two nights, huh?"

"Why, Princess? Have you been missing me?" He quirked an eyebrow, apparently amused. "My cock's been missing you."

"Ryder!" I gasped.

He crawled onto the bed then started kissing up my leg, till he got to my apex. Nuzzling his nose between my thighs, he licked the fabric covering my pussy.

"Hmmm . . . damp . . . sweet and salty . . . Just what I feel like tonight. The taste of you." He shoved the fabric aside and lapped my clit in long strokes. My back arched off the bed as I tried to give him more of me. He pushed two fingers inside. "So fucking wet." I whimpered, my need for him overtaking my common sense as he slid them in and out of me. "All of this is mine. No other man lays a finger on you. Is that clear?"

I nodded, willing him to keep up the work of his expert fingers. He slid the panties down my legs, and pocketed them. "A souvenir for my visit. I will add these to my collection." He grabbed hold of the ends of my nightgown and pulled it over my head. His eyes were glowing as he sucked in a breath. "Jesus, I nearly forgot how fucking beautiful you are."

Both hands glided up my torso, over my ribcage and cupped my breasts. He squeezed hard, making me wince, and then sucked a nipple into his mouth. He bit down on the soft flesh around the nipple, causing me to cry out. Then he did the same with the other breast, biting even harder. Teeth marks left on both breasts.

"If Marcus comes near these tits—my tits—I will kill him. These are mine. Only mine. Got that, Princess?"

"God, Ryder. What are you doing?"

"Marking what is mine. Claiming ownership. Every part of this body belongs to me."

He flipped me over so that I was lying on my

stomach. His mouth was on my ass, as he sucked and nipped and finally sank his teeth into the soft skin, biting hard. "This mark will stay there. Every time you see it, you'll remember whose ass this is."

I gasped as I heard his fly unzip and the rustle of fabric as he kicked off his jeans. Then I heard the tear of foil, before moments later, he rubbed his gloved cock, slick with lube, between my ass cheeks, while pulling my hair so that my head jerked back. With his warm breath on my skin, he whispered in my ear. "And now I'm taking the part of you I haven't owned yet. And you will give yourself to me. I know no other man has been there. I will be the first and the last to claim your ass."

He reached between us and swiped his fingers from my clit all the way to my ass, lubricating my skin with my juices. "Fuck, you're so wet for me, my beautiful bitch." He placed his cock at the entrance of my ass, one hand on my breast, rolling the nipples between his fingers, the other circling my clit as he pushed in slowly, one inch at a time, allowing me to adjust to his cock before going deeper. "Relax, baby," he crooned in my ear, sucking and licking my earlobe so that it sent shivers down my spine. Finally, he was balls-deep into my ass. I couldn't believe how full I felt.

His ownership was never more real than now as he slowly, carefully, started thrusting inside me while squeezing both breasts with every downward stroke, his mouth on my neck, sucking my skin.

I stuck my ass out, wanting him as deep as I could take him, moaning loudly with pleasure and pain. Just as I thought I could take no more, his hand came down on my ass and smacked the skin so that the sound reverberated in the room. Shocked, I shoved backwards, only to feel my ass burn with a second slap. His fingers moved down to my clit, and as he touched me there, biting hard into my neck, I started coming so hard, I thought I'd pass out.

"Fuck, Princess, fuck," Ryder rasped, "you're fucking perfect."

His balls slapped against my ass cheeks as he ejaculated, murmuring into my ear. "Mine. My pussy. My tits. My ass. All mine."

I groaned. "Yes. All yours."

He pulled out and I sank onto the mattress, exhausted, sore, and in ecstasy. I loved being so completely owned and possessed by Ryder.

Ryder spooned behind me, pulling my body against his so that I fit perfectly against him. His chest was heaving as he stroked my skin.

"Good girl," he murmured in my ear. I could hear the pride in his voice, and my heart swelled with joy that I could please him so much.

Finally he settled behind me, cupping my pussy with one hand, the other cupping a breast, his mouth on my shoulder. This was perfect.

I belonged completely to Ryder. He was my man.

CHAPTER 22

JADE

We spent the night like that, Ryder wrapped around me, holding every part of me against him, even as we slept. Exhausted, I wasn't in any condition to ask the questions that were burning in my mind.

I gave in to sleep. It was comforting just being in his arms. I never wanted it to end. But it did—a few hours later, I woke, fully enveloped by Ryder. His fingers on my pussy had wormed their way into my wetness, his thumb rubbing my clit. It was the most delicious way to awaken.

"Baby," I groaned as his fingers inside departed, instantly feeling the loss. But I needn't have worried. His fingers were replaced by a rigid cock, stroking slowly inside me. His thumb on my clit heightened my desire.

The hand on my breast squeezed the nipple hard between dexterous fingers, sending ripples of delight straight to my core. My pussy clenched around his cock, squeezing him back.

Ryder moaned in my ear. "Fuck, baby, what you do to me . . ." He panted as his cock stroked me, the rhythm increasing the longer we were going at it.

My legs were hooked around his, my ass pushing backward, taking as much of his cock inside me as I could. Every nerve ending in my body was receiving pleasure signals, sending me over the edge. I shuddered against him as my orgasm took over, biting my lip so as not to shout out into the silence of the night.

Ryder kept fucking me hard until he exploded inside me with a feral groan, biting into my shoulder to muffle the noise.

First thing in the morning, I was finding that place of my own. The place Ryder could fuck me senseless and I could scream his name without worrying about being heard. It was time. *I wanted it all.* Every orgasm, every thrust of his cock, giving in to the pleasure with abandon, screaming without restraint.

It was time to find *our* place.

We lay like that, silent, spent, the cool breeze caressing our skins, the only light in the room from the moonlight as the curtains billowed. Ryder stayed inside me and I wanted him there so I lay very still, savoring the feeling of him surrounding and filling me.

This was pure bliss. I wanted it every day for the rest of my life.

"Ryder? Can we talk?"

He pulled out of me, fluid spilling all over my beautiful Egyptian sheets. But I couldn't have been happier. I'd rather have Ryder's cum all over my sheets than no Ryder at all.

I turned and buried my face in his chest, inhaling his scent deeply. I loved how he smelled—manly and deeply arousing. I was tempted to lick his nipple ring, but I managed to rein my renewed desire in so that we could talk, because if I started tasting his skin, I wouldn't stop till I'd licked his cock clean.

"What's wrong, Princess?" he murmured, as if he was afraid of my answer.

By now I knew that I had to get straight to the point with Ryder. There was no preamble or easing into a topic. "Tell me why you ended up in juvie. What happened?"

He sucked in a breath. I felt his heart racing beneath my fingertips. Oh God, what had I done? I'd ruined the moment . . .

"We don't always grasp other people's pain, Ryder. Just because we can't see it, doesn't mean they aren't hurting. I want to understand you—and why you are wounded so deeply."

He pressed a kiss into my forehead, but stayed silent. I didn't move because I was afraid that I'd opened a door that should've stayed locked. Eventually he started speaking, his voice low and sad. His story started off slow, with long silences in between, but I stayed quiet, listening, only encouraging him with my fingertips brushing over his skin.

My biker man told me a story of horror. A story of a young boy who'd been deserted by his mother and not understanding why. A boy who protected his baby brother by being willing to sacrifice his own life. I trembled in his arms, tears streaming down my face, unchecked, as he told me how he'd killed a man—his own father—to save the battered body of his little brother. How he wasn't sure, even when he was in detention, that Max had survived, and that taking Tiny's life had meant Max got to live.

He'd lived with that guilt for years, taking the punishment dealt out by the bullies in detention as his penance for what he'd done. He even figured that if Max had died after all, it was his fault for not killing Tiny sooner—for being afraid.

My heart broke, little by little for the boy that was Ryder Knox. His pain was so much more than mine could ever be yet he wasn't bitter. He had tried all these years to make things right by being a wonderful brother to his new family.

When he got to the part of how he was raped by the older boys, how they were going to kill him that day, on his birthday, how they slashed his face and he nearly lost an eye, I was sobbing uncontrollably. Now it was Ryder soothing me, telling me softly that everything was OK.

His story continued. He told me how Cobra and Razor had saved him. How, if it weren't for them, he wouldn't be here today. I sent up a silent thank you to the gods for sending the Malone brothers into the bathroom for a pee that day, just in time to save Ryder from an agonizing end.

My fingers stroked lightly over the scar on his face. Even though it had faded over the years, the physical scar was nothing like the deep internal scar that stayed with Ryder. I reached up and kissed his brow on the spot where the scar had parted the skin and never completely knitted together again. It was even more endearing now that I finally understood where he had gotten it. It wasn't from a fight, or from him being a rough-necked bully as I'd assumed when I first noticed it. No, it was inflicted on a young boy that should never have lived through shit like that.

Shame washed over me. I had judged Ryder on that first day without knowing his story. How quick we were, as humans, to think the worst of one another, never giving someone a chance to prove us wrong. So wrapped in our own egos that we couldn't recognize a fellow human's pain. So quick to jump to incorrect conclusions.

"Ryder, I'm so sorry. I had no idea how much pain you went through," I whispered.

He let out a long, slow breath. "It's nothing compared to the pain that is waiting for me."

I held his cheeks between my palms, staring at his face. His eyes were hooded; I couldn't see in the darkness. Fear gripped my heart. Something was coming that I wasn't going to like.

"Baby, I came tonight to say goodbye."

"No. Please—"

He placed a finger over my lips. "Hush, Princess. You must be strong. For both of us."

"Why, Ryder? Are you going away?" My breath hitched. "*Don't you want me?*" My bottom lip started to quiver as I fought back the tears. I'd just worked out that the feeling I'd felt was indeed love. *Yes, I loved Ryder.* With all my heart. My heart, body, and soul belonged to him. And now he was ending it. It was as if he had stabbed me with a knife and was twisting it in my heart, killing me slowly.

"Baby," he rumbled from deep in his chest, "I want you more than I've ever wanted anything in my life. More than the fucking air I breathe. But it can't work between us. You warned me from the start, and you were right. I know that now. Too many people are going to get hurt, including you. I can't do that to you."

"No Ryder, you're wrong. I'll hurt more if you leave me now. I'm not beyond begging, I'll do what—"

His lips swallowed my words. Why did it feel like it was the last kiss I'd ever get from his mouth? Panic swept through me as I poured every atom of love into my kiss, hoping to God that he'd understand how much I needed him. *How much I loved him.*

"I'm a worthless piece of shit. I've told you my story, so now you know. I'm a criminal—a killer, babe." His voice dipped as he spoke the words. He was fighting for control. "I can never be worthy of you. I can never give you the life you deserve. As much as I hate the thought of you with Marcus, your parents are right. He is the best man for you. He can give you everything you need that I can't."

"You're wrong. So wrong. Marcus can never give me what I need or want. I want *you*, Ryder."

"Princess. You deserve so much more. Everyone is right. Even Harrison. I'm not good enough for you. And being with you places your life in danger. There are people who want to kill me. Well, after tonight, I'll be an empty shell, so they can give it their best shot. But I will never place your life in danger. I just won't."

"I'm begging you, Ryder. Please don't do this."

He grabbed my arms and shook me. "Do you think I want to do this? Fuck, now I've found what I've been looking for all my fucking life? Do you have any idea how hard this is?"

He let go of me so suddenly that I fell back against the pillows as he jumped off the bed. He grabbed his jeans and pulled them on, his jaw clenched with determination.

"I've been grappling with this for fucking days now. Since the night your brother came to the compound. Since Cobra told me to let you go. Fighting every instinct in my body to run away with you."

"Yes. Yes, let's do that. Fuck everything. Let's run away," I said, hope grabbing hold of me for the first time since he'd said the word goodbye.

He laughed, a bitter, sad laugh. "Oh, Princess. And after a while, when you grow tired of me? When I can't give you everything you deserve? What then? You will grow to despise me—even *hate* me." Like a lion in a cage, he paced the room. I held my breath, watching him get a grip on his emotions. He stood in front of the window, staring out into the darkness. With his back turned to me, it was hard to know what he was thinking. My heart ached for him. And for me. How could I make him believe that all I wanted was *him*?

His voice floated across the room. "It's better this way. We're from different worlds, and they can never intercept one another. Trust me on this—its best to say goodbye."

The bed dipped as he sat on the edge to pull on his socks. I crawled to the end of the mattress wrapping my arms around his torso, hugging him from behind. My heart was breaking, but there was nothing I could do to stop him. I knew he was stubborn. Tenacious. The more I begged, the more he'd be certain it was the right thing to do.

"Baby, I'll let you go because I know you're struggling with this. And you won't be ready to accept my love till you've figured it out. I love you Ryder." I stroked his chest with my fingertips.

"I'm no good for you," he murmured.

"You, Ryder Knox, are a brave man. You were a fearless boy who grew up to be a spectacular man. A man worthy of love and happiness. And certainly worthy of my love." Pressing my palm against his heart, I could feel it beating wild and fast.

I had to convince him that I wasn't judging him. "Your heart is *good*, because even though you did terrible things, your intentions were right. If placed in the same position, anyone who loved their brother as much as you do would've done the same."

His gruff voice had a hard edge. "I killed a man."

How could I melt his resolve? I let out a long slow breath, steadying my nerves as I continued. "Don't be so hard on yourself. Often, we are our own worst enemy." I closed my eyes and placed my cheek on his back. "We're hardest on ourselves. Even when others are willing to forgive us, we still beat ourselves up. It's human nature."

"Bitch, you don't know what you're saying." His voice was hard, cold, even. I knew he was hurting so badly that he needed to put up this front.

"It's OK, Ryder. You can pretend you don't love me, but I know better. You're just trying to protect me. It's what you do best. And I love you even more for it. I believe in you."

He sucked in a breath.

"I know we can make it work. All we need is *love*, and one another. I need nothing more than that. I don't need material stuff. I need the love of a man who worships me. That's what I want. *You*, Ryder."

He stiffened. Although he wasn't saying a word, I prayed that he was taking it all in. He had to know how I felt about him, especially after divulging his past. He was damaged, and I wanted to help him heal. I'd spend the rest of my life helping him mend.

"I'm not giving up on you. Ever. Take the time you need, go ride your bike to wherever." Was I really telling him to go away? It was the *last* thing I wanted him to do. I sighed, weariness overcoming me. If only he wasn't so stubborn.

"Listen to your heart. It never lies. It knows all the answers. We were brought to one another for a reason—our worlds collided because we belong together. I love you, Ryder Knox. Everything you are— the good and the bad. I want nothing more—only your love. When you're ready, I'll be here. Because I'm *never* giving up on us."

He loosened my arms from around his waist and rose from the bed. He stood over me, looking down, his gaze drifting over my naked body—the body he had just fucked and was now rejecting.

His eyes were hard. "Princess. You're wrong. *I don't love you.* You're a good fuck, I'll admit that much." His lips pulled into a snarl. "But I tire quickly of fucking the same woman. You were nothing more than a challenge. I needed to break that haughty uptight bitch down to size. Now I've done that, I'm satisfied." He licked his lips.

All I could do, was stare at him, stunned. My blood ran cold.

"Go marry Marcus. He's what a bitch like you deserves. I'm out of here. Thanks for the fuck tonight, I'll put your notch on my bedpost."

How could he be so cruel? The stabbing pain in my heart was unbearable. I clutched the sheets in my fists, recoiling from his words.

He laughed bitterly as he pulled his tee over his head and disappeared from my bedroom, the same way as he had appeared. Unexpectedly.

If Ryder's intention was to shred my heart as payback for judging him, he'd done a damn fine job of it.

I was broken. Empty. *Shattered.*

By Ryder Knox—the man I loved with all my heart.

How fucked up was that?

CHAPTER 23

RYDER

Razor slammed his fists on the table. "Fuck no! I don't accept this shit. This is a truckload of crap and you know it." He glared at his brother, nostrils flaring, fists balled as he challenged Cobra. "I won't have some smartass cop dictate my fucking life. No, and fucking hell no!" he roared.

When Razor got mad, it was futile to attempt to calm him. It only fueled his anger. Besides, I was just as infuriated as he was. Brother's bitches were always welcome at the clubhouse and compound, and now Cobra and the other patched members wanted to place a ban on new women coming in. They may as well have named them directly.

We all knew it was Jade and Lexi that were the problem. All because of Jade's fucking snooping brother.

"Razor. Reel it in, man. It's best for the club. For everybody." Cobra gave Razor the death stare. He was asserting himself as president, and final decision-maker. "Sit down. Both of you." He grumbled at Razor and myself. I hadn't even realized I'd risen from my chair, I was that worked up.

Cobra sighed. "It's because Summers interfered with the weapons deal we had going with the Northern Commando MC that it went fucking sour. My informant also said Summers initiated the fucking raid by the LA Demons. Motherfucker has a death wish. He was trying to get the two MC clubs to fight one another in the hopes we'd wipe each other out, and save him the trouble."

"I say we put a hit on the motherfucker. It's time to get rid of him." Razor's solution to most obstacles was simply to get rid of the source of the problem. It usually worked for him, too.

Drawing in a breath, I shook my head. "No. We can't."

Fuck. Months ago, I would've volunteered to be the fucking hit man. To cut him and let him bleed, slowly, for causing Cobra's near death. But now . . . now that I knew that the motherfucker who was undermining all our club plans was Jade's brother, I couldn't allow it to happen.

If only Summers were transferred to another division, if only he wasn't Jade's brother, and if only he wasn't poking his fucking nose into club business.

Even though I'd given Jade up, vowed never to see her again for her own safety and for my sanity, I knew it would crush her if her brother got killed. I couldn't cause her that loss, and that immense pain after everything she had been through.

There had to be a better way. I had to find a way around this that didn't mean that Harrison Summers had to die.

It was fucking complicated. Since Jade had told me the story, I understood why the motherfucker was so hell-bent on stopping our arms deal. And why he was as hard on the LA Demons and Northern Commando MC as he was on our MC. I even agreed that he had a fucking death wish. But I wasn't going to be the one finishing him off. No fucking way.

Razor removed his switchblade knife from its holster and started cleaning his nails with the sharp point. "I don't care that we have to get a new bar bitch. That's fine. But I want Lexi to be able to come to the club at any time."

"Yeah. Me too." Ox spoke up for the first time since the meeting had started. "Boss, have you forgotten that it was Lexi who actually saved the day when Summers and his squad came to the compound? If she hadn't stayed behind to diffuse the situation with her cousin it could've gone off a lot worse. The fuckers would've turned the place upside down. You know they thrive on that shit. How many TVs have we had to replace over the years 'cause those fuckers get their kicks out of smashing our stuff?"

Watching in amazement, I chuckled—Ox and Razor were actually in agreement for once. They were both sweet on Lexi, that much was clear. But that only meant a different kind of war going on inside the club walls.

Brother to brother. Fuck.

As his VP, I had to stay on Cobra's side. "Yeah, Lexi was smart to not make a getaway with Jade and Ratbag. I was surprised as fuck that she stayed. That does say a lot about her loyalty to the club. But, I also see where Boss is coming from.

We can't risk Summers and his trigger happy bunch of fuckers coming back to look for them. Christ, that just gives him the opportunity to snoop. We provide the reason—he's gonna take it."

Ox's jaw dropped in surprise. He'd seen Jade leave my room that day, because nothing escaped Ox's watchful eyes. And he knew we'd been fucking like rabbits in there. His wink over the pool table later that evening confirmed that he knew Jade was my woman.

"Huh? Ryder—you don't want your bitch to come over? What's wrong with you man?" Razor groaned. He'd bargained on me being on his side in this argument.

I shrugged. "Jade's no longer my woman. I gave her up. It's just better this way."

All eyes were on me now. Even Hammer, who was usually fiddling on his phone during meetings because he was bored, gave me his full attention. They knew I didn't give up easily if I wanted something. I could read the surprise on every face.

"Fuck, brother. *What happened*?" Hammer asked. Of everyone, he knew how invested I was in Jade. He'd helped me do research on her and Marcus's relationship when I thought she was going to go for the douchebag. Hammer was the one who'd told me about the party that night, when I just 'happened' to be there for Jade when she came rushing out.

It was no fucking accident that I was there. I'd been stalking her for days, trying to decide what my next move would be, when she came storming from the building, shoes in hand, bewildered and in need of a dark knight to save her.

When I realized what had happened and that she was running away from her so-called boyfriend, I couldn't have been happier. I wanted to punch the fucker in the face, but he was screwed anyway. The bit I'd gotten to know about Jade, I knew she wouldn't want him. And that's why I decided to take her up Mulholland

Drive. My time to claim what I wanted had finally arrived.

And then, after finding happiness I didn't even know was possible, I had to let her go. Fuck. My heart ached so much that I wanted to ask Razor to cut it out with the pointy edge of that knife he was playing with now. Yeah, I didn't want to feel this pain. Fuck, I was better off being a fuck-'em-and-leave-'em kinda guy.

I shrugged, shifting uneasily in my seat. "Don't want to talk about it. All I can say is that I'm going for a long ride. I'll be gone for around five weeks. I'll go up north and talk with the Northern Commando MC. Give me time to clear my head, and work toward fixing the shit that went down."

The only way I was going to be able to stay away from Jade, as promised, was to put physical distance between us. I may as well be useful while getting out of LA. A trip up the coast to Seattle on my bike was just what I needed. The Northern Commando MC was based in Tacoma, and things needed to be smoothed over.

"I'm coming with you, brother." Before I could even reject his offer, Ratbag added, "I'll be quiet. You won't even know I'm tagging along."

I nodded, grateful for the company, but I also knew Ratbag well enough to know he yakked worse than any woman. Yet I was grateful that I wouldn't be alone. His unending nattering would keep my mind off Jade. I could only hope.

Loving someone the way I loved Jade wasn't for sissies. The real thing was way more painful than the indifference I'd always felt.

I'll never be the same old Ryder again.

Jade had changed me, little by little as she consumed my body, my mind, my heart and now—my soul.

It was because I loved her so much that I had to let her go. It didn't hurt any less. I mourned the loss of receiving her love.

Yeah. I was truly fucked now. I loved the one woman I could never have.

Our worlds had crashed, and it was ripping us apart.

CHAPTER 24

JADE

I managed to get through the fourth week without Ryder. Mia had been kind enough to let me know that Ryder had left for Seattle earlier and would be away for just over a month at a minimum. Maybe even longer, she'd said, because when bikers took to the road, there wasn't any guarantee that they'd be back any time soon. Damn Ryder. He was trying to get distance between us, thinking that would solve our problem. We couldn't even talk to one another. He'd turned his phone off—if anyone had a message for him, it had to go through Ratbag.

I'd had a few conversations with Ratbag, trying to get Ryder to speak to me, but every time Ratbag let me know very apologetically that Ryder had gone silent and wasn't talking to anyone—not even to him.

If anyone had told me what torture it was to be separated from the man one loved, I wouldn't have believed them, at first. It hurt like hell that Ryder didn't even want to speak to me. Just that one small thing—hearing his voice—would've made it so much more bearable.

What was even worse was that I didn't even have a photograph of Ryder. I remembered how he felt, how he smelled, even his crooked smile. But the memory of what he sounded like was fading, and I was panic-stricken by the idea that I couldn't remember his deep, soothing voice that melted my panties every time he spoke to me.

"Jade, honey, I really don't understand why you're moving out of the family home right now, just to be in an apartment by yourself." Mom wasn't happy that I'd found my own place so soon. I'd used some of my investment money as a deposit and bought a cute two-bedroom apartment only a few blocks from Daddy's offices. At least I had a totally valid reason—that I'd be closer to work. Because I was working longer and longer hours just to exhaust myself completely so that I'd tumble into bed at night and drift off to sleep from sheer exhaustion, and not be able to dwell on my dilemma with Ryder. While he was away, it was completely out of my hands—there was absolutely nothing I could do about it, so there really wasn't any point in banging my head against a brick wall.

"Mom, it's exciting to have my own place. Isn't that what you taught me all these years? To be independent, and stand on my own two feet? Well, that's exactly what I'm doing."

"Mmmm, I just never thought you'd use that advice against me. You're hardly eating as it is, so how do I know if you're going to take proper care of yourself?"

"You won't. Unless we catch up for dinner on the weekends. It's time to lose a few pounds of baby fat anyway. My birthday is in a few weeks, and its time I shake off my little girl image."

What Sylvia Summers didn't know was that I was looking forward to just moping around my apartment by myself, with a large tub of ice cream and my favorite book boyfriends. I could stay in my pajamas all weekend without anyone telling me it was unhealthy for a twenty-two-year-old woman to hibernate like that.

Besides, if anyone else tried to fix me up with his or her best friend's son, or organize another blind date, I'd freak the fuck out. If I couldn't have Ryder, I didn't want anyone else. I'd have my career and my novels to keep me going. Real life sucked, anyway. Nothing worked in my favor—I was disillusioned and alone. What I'd always dreamed about: a mansion with a pretty garden, servants, an adoring but successful and wealthy husband, and maybe a grandchild or two to keep my parents happy, was no longer important to me.

I'd be happy with nothing other than Ryder's company, and his love to keep me warm.

But he doesn't love me.

He used me to get revenge on my kind: upper-class snobs that looked down on the less fortunate, including biker types. He wanted to teach me a lesson, and boy, did he ever. I was nothing more than a challenge and a willing fuck to him. Now it was game over.

I'd lost.

Not only were my lifelong dreams shattered and disintegrated, but I'd lost the challenge against the rugged biker, and also the love of my life. Without a doubt, I could never feel for another man what I felt for Ryder. He'd snuck up on me, invaded my being, and now he was so much a part of me that I struggled to function without him.

When my phone rang, I wasn't even curious as to

who was calling. It wouldn't be Ryder. I'd come to accept that by now. He had drawn into his shell, and wasn't coming out any time soon.

It was Rebecca.

"Hey, Jade. I'm coming to visit next week. I'm flying out of Germany on Thursday night, which means I'll be in LA by Friday. So if you want to organize a girl's night out for Saturday, it will be great. I've been working so damn hard that I've hardly had time to socialize. Invite a few of your girlfriends, too, if you want."

I really wasn't in the mood to go out with anyone. I'd rather be alone in my new apartment, but I'd promised Rebecca that I'd entertain her while she was here. My cousin had been through some tough times herself. I wondered what had happened between her and the Frenchman, Alain—if they ever managed to patch things back together? She'd also told me all about her pesky but very handsome boss, and how he was trying to get into her panties although he was a married man.

Why are matters of the heart always so damn complicated?

It appeared that both Rebecca and I had bad taste in men, and that we fell for the wrong guy.

"Ha ha. Believe it or not, I don't have a lot of girlfriends. I'm always either studying or working or reading. I was never part of the *in* crowd at school or at university."

"That's funny, because if it weren't for my two sisters, I'd also be stranded without friends. What about Cousin Lexi? I know we've never been close, but I'd love to see her, too. Can you invite her along?"

"Sure, I will. Lexi is always nagging me to go out. She'll be happy to take both of us to her hangouts. I'll let her suggest where we should go. Is that OK with you?"

Rebecca laughed. "Of course. Why not? If she knows LA better than both of us, she can take us to a club where we can just have fun. God, I haven't done that for so long. It will be awesome just to go a little wild."

"Go wild, you say? *Right.*" I laughed. My idea of a fun night out was movies and popcorn, and back in bed by ten so I could read before going to sleep.

"Dammit, Jade, we're young, and not too shabby looking. It's time we have an evening out on the town. Get a super sexy outfit; we're going to dress to kill, and have a night out that will make history!"

I sighed. Rebecca was beautiful, with her long auburn hair and stunning body. Most men couldn't keep their eyes off her. No wonder she had her boss pining after her. As for the Frenchman—Alain was a damn fool.

Lexi. Well, she was...interesting. She had a banging tight body, and the same beautiful lily-white skin as Rebecca and I. But Lexi was different—she wasn't afraid of her sexuality, or to show off her assets. She changed the color of her hair like other women changed lipsticks. But the weird thing was, regardless of whether she had dark or blond hair she was stunningly beautiful.

Once I'd finished taking to Rebecca, I rang Lexi and told her about our Australian cousin's visit to LA. We hadn't spoken since that night Ratbag had smuggled me out of the compound, and she'd stayed behind. I still wondered about her motives for staying. What man had she set her sights on? I hoped it was Razor or Ox, because Ryder was already taken.

And then I remembered. He'd left me, because he didn't love me.

But that didn't stop me from thinking about him, yearning for him, missing him.

Or loving him. Damn.

CHAPTER 25

RYDER

Two things brought me back to LA sooner than I'd wanted. The first was a call from Max, reminding me that his woman was coming to LA, and that I'd promised to look out for her. He expected me to do some low-profile stalking, ensuring her safety.

Was he also worried that there may be another man in Rebecca's life? I'd heard about the French man she was seeing while she'd been in France, but as far as I knew it was over between them. Maybe Max was worried that he'd try to contact Rebecca on neutral ground? Whatever his reasons were, he was adamant that I had to follow her and be her unknown bodyguard at all times. Fuck, I really wasn't in the mood to babysit anyone, but he was so persuasive that before I knew it, I'd promised to do everything he asked.

The second thing that brought me back prematurely was a call from a man who wanted to meet with me as soon as possible. It had something to do with Marianne. Fuck, I'd nearly fallen off my chair when he'd mentioned her name. He wouldn't tell me anything more, so I agreed to meet him. I was curious as all hell. Why had this happened now, just when I'd finally stated making progress by thinking less of hating my mother?

If I was totally honest, the third thing that brought me home was my longing for Jade. Just being in the same city would be enough for me at this point. Fuck, I missed the shit out of her, even her snarky ways, her witty comebacks, the way she scrunched her nose when she was deep in thought. Yeah, I missed everything about her, so much it hurt. But I'd chosen this path, so I had to fucking suck it up.

However, I did plan on doing some stalking of my very own. I'd be her shadow, and even if she didn't know it, I'd watch over her. *Protect her and keep her safe.*

My discussions with the Northern Commando MC hadn't gone as well as I'd hoped. I was pretty skilled in negotiating, yet we couldn't reach a compromise that would benefit both parties. The motherfuckers were cagey, and wanted more reassurances than I was able to provide to get the deal back on track.

Cobra was raging mad when I called him and told him about their terms and conditions. He shouted down the phone at me, unhappy that I couldn't smooth things over. But what shook me to the core was when he asked me if my heart had been in the negotiations. I couldn't give him a straight answer, because I fucking knew it wasn't. Fuck, I was letting the club and my pres down. That didn't sit well with me.

The Scorpio Stinger MC had always come first in my life; my brothers were my family. And now that had all changed. My thoughts were constantly turning around a beautiful golden-haired woman who'd cast a spell on me.

No amount of wind in my hair or distance on my bike could rid my mind of her. The faster and more reckless I became on the road, and the wider Ratbag's eyes grew, the more I yearned for my Princess bitch. My cock fucking ached for her at night, dying to be buried inside her sweet pussy.

I could only laugh at myself now. How I'd thought running away would help, I had no idea. But I'd tried. It was funny as fuck.

Ratbag thought I'd completely lost my mind when I started laughing uncontrollably for no apparent reason, because it finally dawned on me. No matter how much physical distance was between us, she was always right there with me, wherever I went, because she was in my fucking mind and in my fucking heart.

I could run, I could be in denial, but I couldn't hide from my true feelings.

CHAPTER 26

RYDER

The man standing in front of me was a mirror image of myself, just older. It was like traveling into the future and seeing what I would look like when I was about thirty years older.

"Ryder? Ryder Knox?" Fuck, even his deep baritone voice sounded like mine.

Scrunching my eyes up, I stared at him, trying my fucking best not to gape. *Who the fuck is this man?*

I kept my voice even, hiding my alarm. "Yeah?"

"Christ. You look just like me. It's like looking in a fucking mirror thirty years ago." We even *thought* the same. He shook his head, visibly rattled. His skin was ashen grey, his lips drawn into a thin line. Even the way he stood, fists clenched, legs slightly apart, was a mirror image of myself right at this very moment.

"So—who the fuck are you?" I growled. This shit was shaking me up, and I had no idea why this man was looking for me.

"Listen, Ryder. I need a drink. A stiff one. Can we go somewhere to talk?"

I nodded my head. *Fuck*, I needed more than a stiff drink. I needed to sit as well. For the first time in years, my legs were wobbly as hell. Whatever was going on here would affect my life profoundly.

"Yeah. There is a bar across the road. Let's go there."

"I'm sorry, I didn't introduce myself. I never thought I'd react like this. I was expecting this, but fuck me, it's more bizarre than I thought." He hesitated for a beat, scrubbing his face. A fine layer of perspiration covered his brow.

He extended his hand. "My name is Bill."

I took his hand, looking him in the eyes as I shook it. "You have a last name, Bill?"

"Yeah. It's *Ryder*. William Ryder."

He could have kicked me in the nuts, and it would've had less of a punch to it. "Who the fuck are you?" I hissed. It was no fucking coincidence that we looked alike, and had the same name. And he'd said on the phone that he knew Marianne. That was the only reason I'd agreed to meet him in the first place.

"I'm your biological father." His voice cracked ever so slightly.

All the air had been sucked out of the room. I couldn't breathe. This guy was a nut-job.

"What the fuck are you talking about? My father was Tiny...Steve Mayfair, from Karma Electric. My mother's name is Marianne Knox. You've got your facts wrong, old man." I gasped.

"Ryder. Let's get that drink first—we both need it. It's a long story. OK?"

I nodded. This was going to be interesting as fuck. I

needed to hear what *William fucking Ryder* had to say. Even though I knew he was wrong, I still wanted to hear his story. And fuck, I needed a drink. More than one, actually.

We made our way across the road, silent in our thoughts. Yet, oddly, it wasn't uncomfortable. I didn't warm to strangers easily, but somehow this one had hooked me.

"Two Jacks. Two beers," Bill ordered when we got to the bar.

The barman placed the drinks in front of us. We both lifted the scotch and gulped it down. Damn, that burned. I wiped my mouth with the back of my hand and indicated to the barman to refill the glasses. They went the same way. I picked up my beer and walked to an alcove. I needed to sit.

Bill followed me, sitting across the stained table. My stomach churned. It wasn't only because the joint reeked of stale beer and cheap perfume.

"Fuck. It's uncanny—the resemblance. Marianne was right."

"Marianne?" I sucked in a breath. Jesus, I was feeling sick.

"Your mother. My lover. We were having an affair." He held up two fingers to the barman. Fuck, I needed the whole bottle, not just a shot.

"Who was Marianne *not* fucking? The whore sure got around." His eyes narrowed at my words, a smirk on his face, as if he didn't like what I was saying. I didn't care—it was the truth, and nobody knew it better than I did. I stared at him for a long minute. He looked so familiar, but not only because he looked like me. I'd seen his face and heard his name before. All those music magazines I'd read when I was a teenager—his picture and name were all over them. Why had I never picked up on that before?

I took a sip of my beer. "So. You knew Marianne. That doesn't prove a fucking thing."

He ran a hand through his hair, the exact same dark color and thick texture as mine, although his was short and graying on the sides.

"Ryder, I know it's a hell of a shock—"

I narrowed my eyes. "Are you the William Ryder I think you are?" My hands were clammy, and my heart beat erratically in my chest.

"Which William Ryder would that be?" He raised an eyebrow, sneering. This son of a bitch was as cynical as I was.

"The fucking head honcho of Ryder Music. *That one.*"

He nodded. My eyes burned into his. There were so many questions, I didn't know where to start.

I'd always suspected that Marianne had named me after the music mogul—she was a groupie, after all. But I had no idea she actually knew him, let alone had fucked him.

The barman sauntered over with the bottle to refill our glasses. I took the bottle of Jack from his hands and took a huge swig of the amber liquid. I needed to stop the churning of my stomach.

"Rich dude here will pay for it," I said, nodding my head towards Will. He nodded, his gaze not leaving my face. The barman shrugged and walked off.

"Start talking, William," I growled. "And explain why the fuck you are only showing up now. Why I never knew all this shit before today. And where the fuck is Marianne?" I slammed my fist on the table. I felt like throwing a few of these cheap wooden chairs around, smashing them to pieces. Then punch something. *Anything.* Including Bill's face.

He held up a hand. "Calm down, Ryder. I'll tell you everything I know. We can take it from there." He let out a long, slow breath.

"I'm listening."

"Put the bottle down. I need you to understand what I'm going to tell you." His voice was deadly calm, yet he looked as if he'd aged ten years in the ten minutes I'd known him.

Bill got a faraway look in his eyes. I could tell he was digging up the past. Fuck. I'd been trying for nearly twenty years to forget that past and here it was, sitting across the table from me, dragging up all those feelings again. I'd thought I had a handle on it, and that I'd buried it so deep inside that it would never surface again. I was wrong. All it took was the mention of Marianne's name for me to feel like the helpless boy again, deserted by his own fucking mother.

"I met your mother—"

My fist hit the table again, harder this time. Bill jumped. His eyes widened.

"Don't call her that. Marianne deserted me and Max when we were kids... to fend for ourselves. She's a whore, not my mother," I hissed. "Anyway, where is the fucking bitch?"

Bill closed his eyes for a minute. His jaw slackened, and he swallowed hard. Fuck.

When he opened his eyes, they glittered brightly. "Marianne died, two months ago. I've been looking for you ever since."

"She's *dead*?" Fucking Christ, this was getting worse by the minute. I'd fantasized about seeing Marianne again. About telling her to her face what a shit mother she was. It was my hatred that fueled me, kept me alive through all the things that had happened to me, because one day I was going to find the whore, and give it to her straight. Now she was gone. *Fuck.*

I grabbed the bottle and took a swig, even though Bill clearly didn't approve. *Well, kiss my ass, mother-fucker.* All this time I'd believed that scumbag Tiny was my father—that I'd killed my own flesh and blood. That kind of guilt weighed heavily on a kid; it was virtually insurmountable. Even the fact that I did it in self-defense and to save Max's life didn't make it any lighter a burden to carry.

And now William Ryder was telling me he was my father?

My head hurt, and my chest tightened.

"Yes. I've been looking for her for years. She was supposed to show up at my office with Randy to sign a new contract. I waited all day. They never came."

My eyes widened. "What do you mean?"

"Marianne had called me, and asked for a favor. She said that Jake had throat cancer, and wasn't going on tour any longer. She'd finally had enough of Karma Electric. She begged me to give her new boyfriend a contract so that she could move you and Max away. She wanted to buy a house, settle you boys. Send you to a normal school." His voice faded away. He grabbed the bottle and took a long swig. Seemed I wasn't the only one having a hard time here.

I rubbed at my chest. My heart was squeezing. "She left with Randy. Never came back. Didn't even leave a fucking note."

"That's because she never intended to leave you. She only went with Randy to sign the contract and find a house in LA. She planned to fetch you and Max the next week."

"Yeah? Well, Max and I are still waiting. She never fucking came for us."

Bill was quiet for a long moment. The sorrow on his

face was palpable. His steel-grey eyes—the exact color of mine—were so pained that I had to look away.

"That's because there was an accident. Randy hit a bus head on. He was killed instantly—wasn't even wearing a helmet. Marianne survived, but barely. She was in a coma for months, and when she finally came around, she'd lost her memory."

"What the hell?" I breathed. My throat tightened, and my hands started trembling. It was slowly making sense why Marianne never came for us. Why she didn't save me from juvie.

Fuck.

Bill cleared his throat. He was having trouble talking. "I was married at the time. Even though I knew about you, I couldn't do anything about it. But signing Randy up with a contract meant Marianne would move closer, and stay in LA permanently. I was planning to get to know you. I'd helped them secure a house, paid the school fees for you and Max." He scrubbed a hand over his face. "Then when she never showed . . . at first I was angry. Thought she changed her mind. That she wanted to keep me from seeing you."

"So, you're saying you didn't know about the accident at the time?"

"No. I had no idea. At the time I was busy with a label takeover—I couldn't risk my career trying to find out what happened. The scandal would have killed my business and my wife. She had bowel cancer and something like that wouldn't have been good for her." He blinked a few times, trying to regain his composure before continuing. "By the time I decided to look for you a few months later, you were no longer with the band. It was all hushed. *Nobody* would talk to me." He fell silent, shrugging his shoulders. "I didn't know you were in juvenile prison. I'm sorry." He choked on the last words, his eyes glittering with tears.

"So you just *gave up*?" My mouth was dry.

"My wife really needed me. Our daughter was taking her illness badly, so I had to help her, too. I had so much on my plate, and I figured Marianne took you boys and went elsewhere with Randy. I got tied up in my own life and business. The perils of a high-flying career and success. " He laughed bitterly, shaking his head, his shoulders slumped.

I nearly felt sorry for the bastard. "So what changed? Why find me now?" I took a deep slug of my beer, and wiped the froth from my mouth.

"Marianne lived in an institution for years. She was practically an invalid. Her memory never came back—until one day, a few months ago. Apparently, out of the blue, one morning she woke up lucid and remembered everything. She told the nurses everything she could recall, and they contacted me immediately. I hadn't changed offices in decades, so I was easy to trace."

"You said that was only months ago. And she's dead now?" I was shaking. My eye twitched below the scar. If William noticed, he didn't let on.

"I went to see Marianne as soon as I could. I'd just buried my wife. Things were pretty messed up."

"Fuck. I'm sorry."

"Yes, she fought the cancer, but in the end it took her. As for your mo—Marianne, I got to her just in time. She had contracted pneumonia, and was very sick. The woman was skin and bone. Nothing like the beautiful, vivacious young woman I had known and remembered."

"What did she say? Could she remember what happened?" I held my breath.

"She remembered everything as if it were yesterday. Yet she had no concept of time. She thought you were still little boys. She made me promise to find you and Max, and to bring you to her. She was so excited to move to the new house, to start a new life. She didn't want to understand that years had passed, that her little boys were grown men. It was painful to watch."

I swallowed hard. All these years, I'd hated Marianne for leaving us—not knowing what had really happened. Making assumptions. Wrong ones that had consumed me, and wasted half of my life.

My thoughts went to Jade. She had been right all along. *I am worthy of being loved.* My mother didn't leave me because she didn't love me. She had no choice in the matter. A fucking accident had taken that from her.

Sorrow built in me—a deep ache in my soul that couldn't be soothed. Sorrow that I'd believed the *worst* of Marianne. Sorrow that I'd never tried to find her and seek the truth. And now it was too late. Just as I was beginning to understand unconditional love. My head pounded as it all sank in.

All those wasted years, feeling resentment and anger swirl in my belly. Pushing Jade away because I was afraid to lose her too. I was a fucking idiot.

With clarity born from a light-bulb moment, I knew I had to fight for Jade, now more than ever. I wanted what she offered. *Unconditional love.* Learning the truth of what had happened to Marianne was the turning point I so desperately needed.

"You spoke about your daughter. If I . . . if you . . . really are my father, then that means I have a sister?" Fuck, Max and I weren't alone after all.

"A half-sister." His eyes were hooded, and he looked even sadder—if that was possible.

"Bill?"

"She wants nothing to do with me. Came to the funeral and wouldn't speak to me. Eva thinks it's my fault that her mother died unhappily."

"Eva. That's a pretty name." It was bizarre finding out about a sister I didn't know existed.

Bill nodded. "She looks a lot like you. Same penetrating eyes. Dark hair. And . . . she's stubborn. Smart too." For a moment a smile flashed across his face. There was no mistaking how much Bill loved his daughter.

Silence fell between us for a few moments before Bill continued. "The guilt about you chewed at me, and I told Vivian everything, about my affair with Marianne that started while she was pregnant with your sister. We discovered the cancer just after Eva was born, so I kept the affair going with Marianne all through Vivian's chemo treatment, too. When Eva found out about Marianne and...you, and my despicable behavior, she moved out of the house and refused to speak to me. She visited her mother during the day when I was at work. Even Christmas—"

I coughed and shifted uncomfortably in my chair. I didn't know what the hell to say to that. We all had our fucking burdens to carry. In spite of being a music mogul, and with more wealth than he probably knew what to do with, William Ryder hadn't had an easy life, either.

Jade's words that night in her bedroom came into my mind: *We don't always understand other people's pain, Ryder. Just because we can't see it, doesn't mean they aren't hurting.* Her words were so true. I'd always imagined that the rich and famous didn't have the same problems that throwaway kids like me had. A wry smile twisted my lips. *Fucking Princess.* She was wiser than I ever gave her credit for.

"After Marianne died, I was even more determined to find you. I'd promised her I would. But it was more than that. Other than the few times I got to hold you as a baby, I never knew you. You are my son. I want to be part of your life."

My brow knitted. Whoa. This was crazy talk. Did the man know who I was? VP of a biker club? Wanted by the cops? Criminal and killer?

There was no redemption for Ryder Knox. It was too late.

Besides, I'd make all the same choices again.

"Bill, your story is touching. But I don't give a fuck. I grew up with the only family I ever knew. The Scorpio Stinger MC *is* my family. They saved my life. Not you and a half-sister I never laid eyes on. Go back to your glamorous lifestyle. I'm sure some pussy will take up the slack soon and bring you happiness."

I got up to leave.

"I'm surprised you didn't change your name. If you hated Marianne so much, why didn't you?"

"Because I am who I am. Changing my fucking name wasn't going to change my fucking life. I don't apologize for who I am."

*****

Shaken by learning that I hadn't actually killed my own father as a kid, I had to reassess my whole outlook on life. The biggest burden I'd carried subconsciously for more than twenty years, was that I was spermed by a man such as Tiny—a brutal monster who could lay into an innocent child, and want to kill him because he was rejected by his mother when she chose other men over him. Even though those choices had nothing to do with the child, the fact that he could take out his vengeance and hatred on an innocent boy like Max frightened me.

149

I'd always wondered, waited for that evil streak to come to the surface, and make me just as evil as Tiny.

Thinking back, I was under the impression that even Tiny believed that he'd fathered me; we'd never bonded, and I'd never felt a connection with the man. From Bill's story, Marianne was aware that Tiny wasn't my father, yet she never corrected him. Or me, for that matter. Why would she have kept such an important thing from me? I'd never know, now that she was dead. I couldn't ask her the millions of unanswered questions that ran through my mind.

Also, I didn't understand what exactly William Ryder wanted from me. Wasn't it too fucking late to try and build a relationship with me? Anyway, once he learned about the life I'd led, it guaranteed that he'd quickly disappear again. And this time, it'd be his choice. I shrugged. Why the fuck was I born under such unlucky stars?

Even worse: why was the universe *still* fucking with me? Showing me what could've been with Jade and with William, and then ripping it from me, and laughing in my fucking face?

I shook my head to clear my thoughts. Some things were never meant to be understood.

CHAPTER 27

RYDER

I checked my phone for the address. Yep, I was at the correct hotel. I whistled through my teeth when I entered the lobby. This was fucking flash. I would feel like a fish out of water if I stayed in a fancy place like this. My little brother had to be raking in the cash to send an employee to stay in a glitzy place like this. I bet it had fucking gold taps and orgy-sized baths, just like the house we'd rented in Beverly Hills.

The staff members were giving me the hairy eyeball. They clearly thought just as I did: that I didn't belong here at all. I'd bet every surveillance camera in the fucking place was staking me out. I bet they were just waiting for me to make a wrong move before they kicked me to the curb.

I sat in a large puffy chair and ordered a beer. There was no crime in that, was there? I took my phone from my pocket and stared at the photo of Rebecca that Max had sent me. Yeah, I could see why Max was so into this woman—except for the flaming red hair, she reminded me of Jade. Especially her smile. It made my fucking balls ache.

The waiter's eyes popped when I said he could keep the change from the fifty-dollar bill I'd used to pay for the beer. That should shut him the fuck up, thinking that because I was dressed in jeans, sported a few tattoos, and had a ponytail, and heavy biker boots that I couldn't afford an overpriced beer in an overpriced hotel. He was, after all, the one working for wages and tips, so I didn't understand why he was so quick to turn his fucking nose up at me.

My ears prickled at the sound of laughter floating across the vast space from the direction of the elevators. *Fuck, I'd know that laugh anywhere.* It sent a pang through my heart as my chest grew tight. Fuck me if it didn't sound just like Jade.

I looked up, and straight into curious green eyes. *Rebecca.* Why had her laugh sounded just like Jade's? The beautiful bitch drew in a sharp breath when she saw me, as if she recognized me. Fuck, Max didn't tell her I was playing bodyguard, did he? I wasn't happy about being her fucking babysitter, but at least he could've spared me the embarrassment of her knowing about it.

Before I could curse Max, she turned away, quickly walking in the opposite direction. How she walked so fast in those ridiculous fucking high heels, I'd never understand. Her legs went on forever. Max would be shitting himself if he saw how short her dress was, and how fucking hot she looked.

Next thing it was me sucking in a breath. Fuck me running, if she wasn't embracing a woman that looked just like Jade.

Fuck; it was Jade.

Dressed to kill in a short dress that hugged her body—*the body that was mine*—in all the *wrong* places, pushing her tits up and exposing her long legs atop equally ridiculously high heels.

She looked so fucking hot, I wanted to grab her by the hair and pull her into the nearest cave and fuck her till she was screaming my name.

Then it hit me: she'd dressed up like this—sexy as hell—for a night out with Rebecca. How did she even know Rebecca? As far as the info that Max gave me went, she had never been to LA before. I clenched my jaw as I shoved my fists into my pockets. *Fuck.* Clearly Jade had moved on. Clearly she wasn't staying home pining for me. Clearly she was ready and willing to pick up men tonight.

Did she have a new boyfriend? Had she listened to me and taken Marcus back? Suddenly I cursed that I'd left LA, and that I'd not kept up with what was going on in her life. I'd assumed she'd be home, waiting for me to come to my fucking senses. What I didn't expect was to see her all dressed up, ready for a night out on the town. Fuck. A jealous rage consumed me, and the concierge jumped when he heard the feral growl I let out. Every primal instinct in my body to rush over and claim her was fighting with my common sense.

If Max couldn't control his bitch, that was one thing. *But my woman?* There was no way in hell I was letting any motherfucker touch her. I wanted to punch all these rich fuckers who were staring at her now, and rip out their fucking eyes.

Rein it in, Ryder. Fuck, I was acting like a jealous out-of-control monster.

My mission tonight was to follow and watch over Rebecca, and keep her out of harm's way. And fuck, if I didn't find Jade when I least expected it. I wasn't ready to see her yet, and especially not like this, as if she had moved on and forgotten all about me. That stung.

"Lexi! Oh my God!" I heard Rebecca scream her name and run toward the sliding door, throwing herself at Lexi. *What the fuck?*

As I watched, my eyes wide, it struck me. If Lexi was Jade's cousin, maybe Rebecca was too? Was it possible? Shit.

Three pairs of killer pins and melt-your-heart smiles, all in the same room, was hotter than most men could handle. But I only had eyes for one woman: Jade. Seeing her laugh with her cousins was great, yet I wanted to be the one she was enjoying herself with.

They hooked their arms into one another and strode out of the hotel lobby, leaving every man watching them wishing he'd been invited along. Fuck, I was going to have my work cut out for me. Maybe I needed a wingman?

I quickly followed them outdoors, ensuring that none of them saw me. I jumped onto my Harley just as they got into a cab and pulled away from the curb. I'd be fucked if I lost them.

We weaved through the traffic. I stayed two cars behind the cab, just in case he'd been watching too many movies, and suspected that he was being followed.

The cab stopped in front of an imposing building with the sturdy bouncers at the door, and the women tumbled out of the vehicle laughing, and clearly in good spirits. I saw Lexi put a hip flask into her purse, and cursed. Fuck; they were already drinking, in the cab no less. I definitely needed backup. I quickly dialed Ratbag's number.

"Brother, I need your help tonight. Come down to

Santa Monica—to that new club that opened last week. Yeah, our new client's place." I nodded my head, even though Ratbag couldn't see me. Funny; only a few weeks ago, before my trip to Seattle, I'd negotiated a protection deal with the new owners of the club. It was tough opening a new club if you didn't have the right people in your corner. There was always someone who wanted such a venture to fail, and they'd go to great lengths to prevent new competition from succeeding.

Over the years I'd seen theft, set-ups with drugs, and even murder. For a relatively small cut of the profits, our MC trained the bouncers, and provided protection to the club and its owners. And, since the arms deal went sour, Cobra had used his smarts to think of different ways to raise money for the club that were less dangerous. Make no mistake, this protection racket was as dangerous as any other job. There were always a few trigger-happy crazies that shot their way out of trouble. I knew the type—greedy and unforgiving. They wanted money and power at all costs. Nothing was sacred, or too high a price for them to pay.

Lexi flashed a card at the bouncers and the burly man opened the door to let the three women straight in. A few boos from the people standing in the long line only made her flash them her ass. Fuck, she was sassy. I watched as she lifted her skirt, exposing her perfect creamy orbs covered only in a neon-yellow thong to the crowd. The guys cheered, wolf whistles filling the air along with throbbing music from the inside of the building. I smiled as one bitch swatted the arm of her man for grinning lasciviously at Lexi's ass. Man, I felt for him, 'cause if it weren't that I was in love with the blond bitch, I'd so tap that sexy ass.

I was in love, not blind...and the way the bouncer guy was grinning at Jade made my blood boil. I recognized the fucker; he was one of our picks for the job. Right now, I wanted to slam him in the nuts for eyeing my girl. I swallowed hard as Jade smiled sweetly back at him and he guided her by the elbow into the club. Fucker. There was no need to *touch* her. My fists opened and closed of their own accord.

"Hey, Ryder. Chill, man." Razor's voice cut through the noise. "Ratbag said you needed some help with some Sheilas. Well, here we are, brother. What a great assignment."

Fuck. Just what I needed. Razor was going to go ape-shit when he saw that Lexi was here, flashing her ass at strangers. I rolled my eyes at Ratbag—didn't he understand I wanted him to come alone?

Ratbag shrugged as if he comprehended my annoyance. "Razor overheard our conversation. He insisted on coming. Said he was going crazy at the compound." Maybe it wasn't such a bad idea after all . . . these three women were going to be a fucking handful.

"Where's the action, brother? I'm ready to meet these bitches." Razor flexed his muscles, and a few single ladies in the line called out to him. Usually I played along, but I wasn't in the mood for Razor's antics. I needed to find the women. I needed to keep Razor on track.

"Hey brother, Lexi's in there, with Jade and Rebecca, my brother's woman. We don't have time for this shit now."

Razor's head jerked up. His eyes narrowed. "Lexi?"

I laughed. All I needed was one word to get his full attention. I quickly explained the whole situation to the guys, and that we should keep a low profile and watch from a distance. He groaned as I made myself clear that we were observing only. Now I knew why I didn't want Razor here—he was hot-headed, and didn't follow instructions easily.

"Clive," I greeted the burly man at the door. He recognized me immediately, and moved over so that we could enter. I liked when a man knew his place.

Once inside, it took a minute to adjust my eyes to the relative darkness. Clive clearly understood why we were here and indicated to the mezzanine level. I looked up, and saw that the women had settled at a table and had ordered drinks. Already, a few men were leering at them. Razor growled again. Fuck, it was going to be hard to keep him calm and in check.

I watched Jade stand by the railing, cocktail in hand, her body moving rhythmically in time to the music. My cock jerked as I imagined being inside her, moving in sync with her. Fuck, she was beautiful, even from this distance. I could see the smile on her face. Rebecca and Lexi joined her, and the three of them started bumping hips, and swaying their asses. Jade emptied her glass and placed it on the table. She meant business. She lifted her arms above her head, closed her eyes and really got into it. Fuck. I'd never seen her dance like that before, and my cock strained against my jeans. I saw the grin on both Razor and Ratbag's faces too. Razor adjusted his cock, groaning as he did.

But we weren't the only men here enjoying the spectacular show. Waiters started appearing with drinks, and gesturing toward surrounding tables. The girls waved in the general direction of their sponsors as they accepted the beverages. *From strangers.* Fuck. Jade was getting the spanking of her life for that once I got back with her. Didn't her parents teach her about fucking stranger-danger? And her cop brother? Jesus. Harrison would have a heart attack if he knew what was going on. Suddenly, I had empathy for the guy. Never having a sister, I didn't have to worry about shit like this.

But then I remembered–*I did have a sister*. OK, a half-sister. All of a sudden, I really wanted to meet her. It came from nowhere, and hit me like a ton of bricks. Yeah, I wanted to meet my sibling—it would be nice to not be the eldest child for a change.

A few more songs in, and the girls had a full audience. Guys were standing around, clapping in time to the music, spurring on the girls to dance even more seductively. I had to hold on to Razor as Lexi grinded her ass against one dude's pelvis. I was sure the fucker was hard, and she seemed to enjoy the show.

What I saw next nearly drove me insane. A tall fucker wearing a cowboy hat strode over as if he owned the fucking joint, and placed his hands on Jade's waist. She smiled up at him seductively, and placed her hands over his as she gyrated her hips in time to the music. I couldn't tear my fucking eyes away. It was sensuous as hell, but it should've been *my* hands on her hips, not some random fucker's.

I was in two minds about what to do, when Cowboy's hands slid up over her ribs, and his thumbs brushed over her tits. Jade's arms slipped around his neck and she leaned in, pressing her tits against his fucking chest. Alarm bells went off in my head, clanging so loudly that it gave me a headache. Jade *liked* the fucking cowboy; she was openly flirting with him. There was no fucking way I was going to be able to stand here and watch it for much longer. Jealously raged through my body, my heart twisting in agony. Fuck.

What would Jade's reaction be if she knew I was here? How would she react? I was more afraid of finding out than of watching, so I just stood there, my insides churning. This was what I had wanted, right? I wanted Jade to find someone who was more worthy of her than me. Wasn't that what I'd told her?

Fuck NO. I couldn't bear it.

From the corner of my eye I saw Razor push to his feet and scramble across the dance floor, shoving people out of his way. I was too late to stop him. Ratbag tried to go after him, but the crowd was too thick, and Razor disappeared amongst a sea of people bobbing up and down. Fuck.

My gaze went back to the mezzanine level... back to the women. My eyes widened when I saw what had gotten Razor so agitated. A large sturdy guy with even more tattoos than Razor, had his hands on Lexi's ass, pressing her into what I assumed would be a raging fucking hard-on, his fucking tongue down her throat.

And Jade? She had her fucking head resting on Cowboy's chest, her eyes closed, swaying to the rhythm of the slow song.

Next thing Razor was taking the steps, two at a time, till he got to their table. Rebecca screeched as she saw Razor storm down on Lexi, her hand over her mouth as terror filled her face. Razor must have looked like one mean motherfucker at this moment. I'd seen his angry face often over the years, and I knew it wasn't pretty. It would scare the living shit out of anyone.

CHAPTER 28

JADE

Hallelujah. The plan we'd hatched in the taxi was working. And it was about damn time, because I was about to punch Cowboy if he licked my ear one more time.

After we'd settled in on the back seat, Rebecca had gone all quiet and deep into thought for a moment, and Lexi, just being herself, started questioning our cousin about it. Rebecca told us about the man she'd seen in the lobby who looked completely out of place, yet she could tell he was there for a reason. What really bothered her most was that he reminded her of her boss, Maxwell Grant. Apparently the similarities in looks were uncanny, and freaked her out a bit.

So when Lexi started interrogating poor Rebecca for more details, we both looked at one another, not believing our ears. LA was a big place, but how many biker-type guys that looked just like Ryder Knox could there be?

We decided to be on the lookout to see if he was following us. My heart nearly jumped out of my damn chest. I wanted it to be Ryder so badly that I wasn't sure I'd be able to contain myself if it really was him.

The taxi driver was on our side. He'd been a rookie cop for six months before his partner was shot, and he consequently decided that kind of life wasn't for him. But he loved the whole premise of us being followed, and the excitement of using his skills to evade our stalker.

He confirmed that a motorcycle was indeed following us. He went roundabout ways, weaving through traffic to shake our pursuer, but the motorcycle stuck to us like shit to a blanket, as Rebecca had put it, bringing us all to tears with laughter. Whoever he was, he was never more than two cars behind us.

When we got to the club, Lexi told me to not look around once we got out of the taxi—under any circumstances. It was also her crazy idea that I should be an exhibitionist tonight and dance seductively to attract men in the club, forcing Ryder—if it was indeed him—to show himself.

Lexi pulled a hip flask of bourbon from her purse and ordered me to drink some of it. It burned all the way down my throat, but it also helped ease the jitters that had come over me.

If it was Ryder, why the hell was he following us? Surely he knew that he we could talk at any time, so why would he feel the need to stalk me? Presuming, of course, that it was *me* he was stalking, and not Lexi or Rebecca. An uneasy feeling churned in my stomach. Maybe Ryder had his sights on my cousin? After all, she was more his type, with her tattoos, and piercings, and foul mouth.

But it would be cruel to chase after Lexi in front of me. Maybe he just didn't care. I sighed heavily, anxious to see Ryder again, whatever the reason for him being here.

"Oh my God, don't look now, *but it is fucking Ryder Knox!* And guess who the fuck just joined him?" Lexi groaned as we got to the entrance. To give her an opportunity to turn around and face where she thought Ryder was hiding out, she proceeded to flash her ass to the crowd.

I had to laugh out loud. It would only be Lexi that was willing to expose herself to strangers for our cause. She laughed and said it was worth it, because none other than Razor, the man she was sweet on, had joined Ryder on the curb.

Razor hadn't spotted her yet, but she was sure it would only be a matter of time before she drove him crazy with her antics and he came to claim her.

I channeled my inner stripper and gyrated my hips, needing to down the drink to numb my mind, because I was feeling like a huge fool—and a tramp. I searched the darkness for Ryder, scanning the booths, trying to see his face as I rocked my body.

But he was nowhere to be seen.

"Bring it, girl." Lexi laughed as she gyrated her ass against a huge raging hard-on belonging to a rather handsome guy. She was enjoying herself way too much . . .

Shit was going to go down tonight. Ryder had told me about Razor's attraction to Lexi, and also about what a hothead he was. Chances were good that the biker boys were going to play beautifully into our hands.

Then Cowboy stepped up and claimed me. Shit. Not the man I wanted right now.

"Work it," Lexi spurred me on. "Pretend it's Ryder."

That helped. I closed my eyes and let the stranger fondle and embrace me, all the time smiling as I imagined that it was Ryder. But when Cowboy licked my ears, I couldn't pretend any longer. What the fuck was taking Ryder so damn long? *Or did he really not care?* Damn, maybe I should just leave with Cowboy, let him take me somewhere, ply me with more alcohol and fuck me. The booze was already working its way through my system, helping me lose my inhibitions.

I hadn't had a man since Ryder had left. It was six weeks, and counting. I was tired of using B.O.B. and I wanted *Ryder* inside me. But if he didn't want me, I'd have to settle for someone else. Peeping through my lashes at Lexi, I squirmed when I saw she'd let the tattooed guy palm her ass, and virtually suck her up with his mouth. She'd worked him into a frenzy, and although it was all part of the plan, my throat tightened. What if our tactics bombed? What if neither Razor nor Ryder came to save us?

My eyes flew open when I heard Rebecca shriek. Razor was storming down on Lexi with a murderous look on his face.

"Shit!" Cowboy mumbled in my ear. "Let's get out of here."

Cowboy must've seen Razor's face, because he'd gone paler that his baby-blue shirt. I looked behind him to see if Ryder was in his wake, but no. *No Ryder.* My heart sank into my pointy-toe stilettos.

"Come, babe, let's go somewhere quiet," Cowboy said and pulled me in the opposite direction to where Razor had come from. Disappointment washed over me as my heart squeezed. If Ryder was here and had seen all of this, he obviously couldn't care less. What if he was in fact chatting up another girl, planning to fuck someone else? *Of course.* I could've slapped myself.

Ryder isn't following me. What an idiot I am.

Following Cowboy, I nearly tripping over my own feet as we left the scene. Cowboy seemed to know exactly where he was going, so I just followed him past the crowd of bodies until we got to a secluded passage at the back end of the club. I was humiliated, sad, and angry, all rolled into one. I needed someone to take my mind off how bad I was feeling.

Cowboy was very handsome. His sandy-brown hair peeked from under his hat, his square jaw was cleanly shaven, and he had bright and intelligent eyes. He was the kind of man I would've gone for—*before* I met Ryder. Clean, wholesome, smart—those were the things that always attracted me to men. So why wasn't I turned on by Cowboy? Had I gone all cold again? What the hell was wrong with me?

We reached a narrow flight of steps that led to a door. Where was he taking me? Slightly out of breath, my heart beat wildly as a mixture of fear and excitement swept through me. We stood on the landing, Cowboy's arm possessively around my waist, as he punched numbers into a keypad. I heard a click and he pushed the door open, pulling me inside.

How did he know what the code was?

Who the hell *was* Cowboy?

CHAPTER 29

JADE

"Wait. Who are you? Where are you taking me?" I gasped. He'd already closed the door behind us. *Fuck.*

"Don't worry your sexy ass about that, babe. My brother and his partners own the place. I help him out. We were watching you and your friends from up here—the security room—when I decided I needed to tap your pretty ass. If you were offering, I was taking." He winked at me, a lascivious grin on his face. "Wasn't letting the other pricks beat me to the prettiest girl here tonight. My brother fancies the redhead, but I want you. You and I will have the room to ourselves, soon. I'll send the boys on a floor-round. That should give us enough time alone."

He pinched my ass, and shoved me toward another door. Through the large, darkened glass windows, I could see the people beneath us. This was a really cool place to check the crowds from without them even knowing. The one-way windows were covered with mirrors on the outside so it looked like décor, not a security office. *Damn.*

"Floor round," he barked as we entered the room. "Thirty minutes, minimum."

The two guys nodded. "Sure, Colt."

"No, please stay," I begged. Shit; I didn't want to be alone with Cowboy. They ignored me. Treating me as if I were thin air, they stuck earphones into their ears and left the room.

"Strip, babe. Take it all off," he commanded.

"Colt? I hardly know you. Can we have a drink, and get to know one another first?" My previous ideas of wanting to fuck a stranger were sounding dumb to me now.

"Why not?" he drawled, his eyes raking my body appreciatively. "The guys won't be back for a while. Plenty of time for a good fuck, huh?" He opened a cupboard and brought out a bottle of bourbon and two glasses. Maybe if I had a few drinks in me, I'd forget about Ryder and let Colt take me, hard, so I could get Ryder out of my system. Yeah, that was exactly what I needed. Another man's cock riding me, replacing Ryder once and for all so that I could move on. The message was loud and clear. Ryder didn't care—he didn't love me, or even want me.

Move on, Jade, the sooner, the better.

"God, you're beautiful. I can't believe you don't have a man."

I narrowed my eyes at him. "What makes you say that? Maybe I do have a man."

"No fucking way would your man let you come to a club dressed like that, putting out like that on the dance floor. You were practically begging to be fucked, and it looked like you wouldn't care if it was right there in front of everyone. And letting a stranger touch you the way you let me touch you . . . I bet your pussy is so wet right now."

Sweet Jesus. When Lexi told me to imagine it was Ryder, I must've let all my longing take over if that's what Colt saw. And why was it so fucking sexy when Ryder spoke to me like this, yet I was offended by Colt's direct ways? What made it different? Dirty talk was dirty talk, right?

Grow up, Jade. Stop living in the past, hoping for Ryder to come back. Do what the women in your romance novels do. Let this hunk of a cowboy ravish you—give you pleasure. Yes, my pussy was wet, but not because of Colt. But why waste that? He didn't have to know about my thoughts, that I was imagining Ryder... that I was wet and throbbing because I imagined Ryder was watching me dance.

"Give me another drink, Cowboy," I said, trying to sound cool and mature. My head was starting to spin, and I even started to relax as Colt stroked up and down my thigh, his hand going higher every time, closer and closer to my pussy. It was a matter of moments before he explored further...

He kissed me, hard and passionately. Colt was in to me. *He* really wanted me. He pulled me into his arms, his raging erection making his intentions perfectly clear. His hand slipped to my breast, and rubbed over the nipple.

"Mmm babe, you feel so soft. I can't wait to taste you," he murmured at my ear as he lifted my dress to my hips, exposing the garter belt and matching thong I wore.

"God, you're hot. That's sexy as fuck," Colt groaned as he stroked over the fabric, feeling my dampness. He spun me around so that I was facing the window, my ass naked to his eyes. My back arched as he stroked the orbs of my flesh before he pushed me forward so that I had to place my hands on the glass to keep my balance. I felt the music vibrate through the glass, the beat of the drums echoing in my heartbeat.

Fleetingly, I wondered what had happened between Lexi and Razor. Was Rebecca okay? I hoped she wouldn't be mad at me for leaving, but I had little doubt that she'd have male company regardless.

I bit into my lip as Colt stood behind me, grinding his erection into my ass while both hands fondled my breasts. *Did I really want this?* Below me, hundreds of people swamped the dance floor—a throng of bodies gyrating against one another. It seemed like a mass orgy moving in time to the music and strobe lights.

My gaze fell on a man, standing with his hands on his hips, totally disconnected from the rest of the mob. He looked so out of place, it was hard to miss him. I sucked in a breath when I recognized him. *It was Ryder.*

The most bizarre thing happened next. Ryder actually looked up, directly to where I was standing, with another man making his moves on me. As if he was drawn to me, Ryder scrunched his eyes, rubbing his chin, staring in my direction. I knew he couldn't see me through the mirrored windows, yet it felt as if he was looking at me.

Colt's hand moved to my groin, but before he could slip his fingers under my panties, I bucked my ass and shrugged him off me.

"Let go, Colt. This isn't happening tonight." I pulled my dress down, trying to regain my dignity.

"Babe," he groaned. "What do you mean? I want this, you sure as hell want this—"

I held up my hand. "Sorry." I shrugged. "It's a woman's prerogative to change her mind."

"Are you fucking serious?" He raised both eyebrows, and his lips drew into a thin line.

"As a matter of fact, I've never been more serious in my life," I replied as I fixed my hair.

"Well, it doesn't work like that around here. Just so you know, I don't take no for an answer. You are a cock-tease; I get that now. What do you want, babe? You want me to beg? Does that get you off?"

With my mouth gaping, I shook my head.

"Ah, you want me to force you, take you rough. Sure, sweetheart, I can fuck you hard. No problem. That's it, yeah?"

My throat went dry. Jesus, I was in trouble. "N . . . no," I stuttered.

He threw his head back and laughed. "Fuck me. I get it now. *Money*. I never thought that's what a classy woman like you would want. How much?" He walked to a drawer and pulled out a wad of cash. "You're lucky you're so fucking gorgeous, and that I'd be willing to pay to fuck you."

Fully aware that the door was locked and I needed a code to get out, I had to play my cards right. "No. I don't want your money—" I stammered. "I just want to leave."

"Pretty baby, that's just not going to happen. I'm hard for you. The more you resist, the more it fucking turns me on. I like fight in my woman. I grew up on a ranch—I like things rough. It going to be fun to tame you, baby. Fuck, yes."

The wad of cash landed on the wooden table with a thud. He rounded the desk, lust burning in his eyes as he closed the distance between us. The circular room was cramped; there wasn't space for me to maneuver, unless I crashed through the glass. However, I had no doubt that would be impossible. This was most likely shatterproof glass. Plus, Colt had positioned himself between me and the door. Even if I knew the fucking code, I still had to get passed him.

"You look so sweet and innocent, but I bet you fuck like a tiger." His top lip curled into a lewd grin. Colt grabbed hold of the fabric at my neckline and ripped the top open with one hard tug. I heard the buttons scatter on the floor.

"Colt. I'm not looking for trouble. I like you; you know that, right? But I'm an old-fashioned girl. I just want to move slower." Panic had risen in my chest, and my mouth went dry. I was going to need every skill in my arsenal to get myself out of this damn fix I'd gotten myself into.

"Tonight you can count on one thing. *I am going to fuck you.* Long and hard, up against the window, so that you can watch the people below us while I make you cum."

"Please, Colt. Let's go down to the club and get a drink. OK?" I would beg if I needed to.

Colt pushed me against the glass, his mouth on my chest, hungrily licking over my skin.

"No. First, we fuck. You've teased my cock long enough. This is a soundproof room. You can scream as hard as you like when I make you cum, because nobody can hear you. Besides, the noise from down there—"

The door burst open. Stunned, both our heads jerked toward the intruder. I could have cried with gratitude. My eyes locked with stormy grey ones. Ryder stood there, fists clenched, his face contorted in anger.

"What the fuck, man? Get your fucking paws off my woman," he roared, ready to punch the cowboy in the face.

With three long strides, Ryder stood in front of me. He looked me over, taking in the ripped top and fear in my eyes.

"Jade. You OK?" he rasped. He didn't touch me. And he called me Jade. Not Princess. Not even bitch. Just Jade.

But ... he'd said I was his woman ...

I just stared at him, at a loss for words. Did he really mean that? Should I be happy he saved me? Again? And how did he know where to find me?

My heart beat wildly in my chest.

His woman.

CHAPTER 30

RYDER

Marcus was a prick. There was no denying that. But at least he was screwing some other bitch. This Cowboy, on the other hand, was trying to screw my woman.

Over my dead fucking body.

"Who the fuck are you? And how did you get in here?" Cowboy yelled, clearly not happy about the intrusion.

A cough from the doorway had all three of us turn our heads. The burly bouncer that had shown us the way into the club was standing there, looking uncomfortable. He shrugged as he tried to explain. "He's from the Scorpio Stinger MC. Ryder got me this job. So when he asked me to open this door for an emergency, of course I complied."

"Well, get the fuck back to your station. *Now.* I'll deal with you later." Cowboy was losing his shit, but I wasn't finished with him yet.

Fisting his shirt and twisting it so that Cowboy's face was mere inches from mine, I growled. "Just 'cause we have a deal with your brother, and because you probably didn't know that this is *my woman*, I'm letting you off this one time. But . . . if I even see you looking in her direction, never mind touching her again, I will cut off your dick and feed it to the birds. Got that, Cowboy?"

On the way up the stairs, Clive had filled me in on exactly who the fucking cowboy was I'd seen pawing Jade. And, luckily for him, he was still fully clothed. I guessed that I'd just made it up here in time.

Not many people would know about this security room, but fortunately, I remembered because Cowboy's arrogant prick of a brother had shown it off when he gave us a tour around the place a few weeks ago. Doing business with the club had paid off.

When Jade just vanished in to thin air, I nearly lost my fucking mind. She'd acted completely out of character dancing like that, so I knew she was alcohol-fueled, and wasn't thinking rationally. And the way the fucking Cowboy was all over her . . . I wanted to fucking make him bleed for that.

But there were more important things to deal with right now. I had to make it right with Jade. I was praying like fuck that she'd take me back—that I hadn't fucked up completely, and that it wasn't too late.

Christ, maybe she wanted Cowboy to screw her, and I was the one out of line here?

I squeezed my eyes shut for a few seconds as I dealt with that possibility. I'd royally fucked up this one precious thing by acting like a dumbass prick. I'd rejected the love she'd offered me, so I couldn't blame her for moving on. But it would hurt like fuck.

"Ryder? Why are you here?" she whispered, her voice hoarse and shaky.

I shoved the cowboy hard so that he staggered backward, landing in a chair. Luckily he was not as dumb as he looked, 'cause he just stayed there, his mouth gaping as he stared at us.

"I came for you, baby." My voice cracked as I said the words. She had to know how I felt about her—that I wanted her with every fiber in my being. That I couldn't breathe when I was away from her.

"You did?" She gasped, her beautiful eyes brimming with tears.

"Yeah." I grinned, feeling like the idiot I was. "Don't want to live without you, Princess. You're what gives my life meaning...makes it worthwhile to get up in the morning. If I ain't got you, I ain't got anything."

I pulled her into my arms and just stared into those pools of blue. I wanted to see the answers there—I wanted to look deep into her soul, and see if she still loved me as much as I fucking loved her. *If she was just as lost without me.*

What I saw made my heart leap with joy. Her eyes shone, not from her tears, but with unadulterated love. Fuck, how did I ever deserve this? A woman as perfect as Jade, loving me? But I would take it, and show my gratitude every day for this blessing that the universe had finally given me, by worshipping her.

"You've got some explaining to do, Biker Boy." A small smile touched her lips. Fuck, she was going to make me pay. My lawyer girl was smart.

Taking hold of her chin, I raised her face to mine. Dipping my head, I brushed my lips over hers. Christ Almighty. This was what I'd been missing. Just the feel of her lips against mine and I was hard for her. She held my heart—and my life—in her small hands. Did she even understand the power she held over me? It would take me a lifetime to explain that to her.

A cough from the chair brought me back to the present. "Fuck me. The two of you are going to set this place on fire if you carry on like that."

"You're fucking lucky I have my woman to take care of, and don't have time to kick your balls right now. Get us a room. *Now*," I barked at him.

Above the club were a few guest rooms for VIP club members. Cowboy's brother—who wore a similar king-sized cowboy hat—had proudly shown them off on our tour. No expense was spared to make them as luxurious as possible, so the prick had been bragging about all their features, including the expansive mirrors on the walls and ceilings.

While I was looking for Jade and Cowboy, I'd prayed that he hadn't taken her to one of the guest rooms. Those would be harder to get into—I doubted that Clive would have the code to get in there. Something drew me to the security room instead. The pull was so strong, I had no choice other than to follow my gut instinct and go there instead of investigating other possibilities.

Had I made the wrong choice . . . I shuddered at the thought.

Hopefully one of the guest rooms was available, because I had to be alone with Jade. It couldn't wait a minute longer. I had to tell her how I felt about her. *Claim her back as my woman.* Yeah.

"It's your fucking lucky night I reserved one of the guest rooms for myself tonight. Take it. I know when I'm beaten." Cowboy was fucking smarter than what I'd given him credit for. He withdrew a key card from his shirt pocket. "Here. Take the elevator to room 314. It's all yours till the morning."

I snatched the white plastic card from his hand and

shot him a warning glance. He was still not off the hook—I'd keep a fucking eye on him, in case he got any ideas that *my Princess* was fair game. I wasn't taking any chances again. I'd learned my lesson the fucking hard way.

CHAPTER 31

RYDER

Beaming from fucking ear to ear, I couldn't take my eyes—or hands—off Jade as we traveled up in the elevator, but I knew I had a lot of explaining to do, and that she wasn't going to let me off lightly. After what I'd put her through, and the agony of still not knowing if she would take me back, I needed answers. I was going to have to bring my A-game tonight.

Jade had agreed to accompany me to the guest room, but that was no guarantee that I was home-free. No, I got the impression that she was that eager to get out of the claustrophobically small security room with the strange view, and that she would have agreed to anything if it meant her freedom.

That's exactly why I was holding on to her arm with a steel-like grip as I steered her toward room 314. She'd bolted before; I wouldn't be surprised if she tried it again. And fuck, I was getting tired of the cat-and-mouse game. I just wanted for us to be together. For-fucking-ever, and be done. The mechanics of how and where were less important than the reason why.

As I swiped the card, she stood at the door, rigid and unsmiling.

"This is a mistake. Thank you for saving me from an asshole again; it seems you are always there just when I need you most. But I must leave now. I just can't do this."

"*Princess*," I breathed, my heart sinking all the way to my heavy boots.

"Please don't stop me. It's best this way." She stood on her toes and planted a soft kiss on my cheek. Then she turned and walked away. The elevator doors were still open, so she walked straight in and pushed the button. Her words had frozen me to the spot.

Please don't stop me. It's best this way.

How could I disrespect her wish? Fuck. What the hell was I supposed to do? Watch her walk away?

Before I could move or say anything the doors closed.

The sadness in her eyes was the last thing I saw. *Fuck.* Did that mean she didn't love me anymore?

Yes, our worlds were completely different.

Yes, we were up against the worst kind of odds—our very own families. Not to mention my own special brand of stupidity.

Fuck that shit.

It was time for Ryder Knox to fight for what he truly wanted. To fight for love, and happiness. To the very fucking end.

If Jade didn't love me anymore, I wanted to hear her say those words directly to me. I was done with the fear of losing her driving me to deny myself what my heart desired most. Why the hell did humans do that to themselves? Christ, I was my own worst fucking enemy.

It took me another ten seconds to mobilize myself. I flew down the stairs, two at a time. I had to stop her. I had to fight for her.

She was my woman, and she was worth fighting for. Hell yeah.

I reached the bottom of the stairs and darted toward the elevator. *Empty.* Fuck.

Frantic, I ran around the lobby, trying to find where she'd gone. There was no time to waste. I needed to stop her, to tell her how much I loved her, even if she didn't love me, so that she could know she owned my heart . . . and my soul.

What she did with that knowledge would be up to her.

Out on the sidewalk, there was nothing but the normal city buzz. My throat tightened when I noticed the cab further down pulling away from the curb. There was nothing I could do. By the time I got to my bike, she'd be far away. I didn't even know where she'd go to. Mia had mentioned in passing that she'd moved out of her parent's home.

I stood there, my heart shredded. Yeah, typical. Just when I'd thought things were looking up, they turned to shit. Why did it always fucking happen to me? I ran my fingers through my hair, suddenly tired as fuck. I was wiped out from the long journey I'd just returned from days ago. Wiped out from lack of sleep and worry. Wiped out that I'd lost the one thing that mattered to me most in life.

I'd lost everything, because Jade was all that I ever wanted. She made me whole.

CHAPTER 32

RYDER

I had finally come to the darkest night in my life. Everything had collided and combusted; only embers were left burning.

Deflated, and tired to the bone, I remembered that in my mad dash to get to Jade, I'd left the guest room door wide open. Depleted, I shook my head and decided to get back up there and sleep off my fatigue, so that I'd be ready to make new plans in the morning. I knew that everything that seemed insurmountable in the darkness of the night somehow wouldn't appear as big an obstacle in the daylight.

Too shattered to care about anything, I rode the elevator back up to the third floor. It'd be too hard to even find my way back to the compound, so I was staying the night. I closed the door. The room was dark, but I couldn't be bothered to find the light switch.

I pulled my boots off my feet at the entrance and

threw them into the corner, and went in search of the bed. I needed to sleep. An exhaustion had come over me, like I'd never felt before. I simply couldn't care about anything now that Jade had walked out of my life.

"Ryder?" Her voice floated softly across the quiet darkness. Fuck. Now I was hallucinating. And I hadn't touched a drop of booze or any substance, which meant that I was in a worse shape than I'd imagined. My eyes slowly adjusting to the darkness, I stumbled against what I presumed was the bed. I needed to lie down and close my fucking eyes.

I fell onto the bed, face first, arms stretched out.

"Ryder!" Her voice was louder; it sounded so fucking real I could scream. Princess was tormenting me, fucking with my mind. At this rate it would be impossible to fall asleep if I kept hearing her voice.

A soft hand on my shoulder made me jump. *Fuck!*

Never having believed in ghosts, I grabbed blindly in the direction of the voice, only to hear her laugh softly. I was definitely losing my mind. Jesus fucking Christ.

"You're crazy," the sweet voice whispered. Fuck, I couldn't agree more. I was positively certifiable.

Her soft curves pressed into my hard body. I could even smell her. If this was indeed a dream, I didn't want to wake up. Ever.

"Go to sleep, baby, you're so tired. Just go to sleep," she whispered as she stroked my hair. Somewhere between consciousness and sleep, I knew this was real.

So this is what an out-of-body experience feels like.

She was here. I didn't know why or how. She was holding me, caressing me.

Loving me.

I was home.

*****

181

I woke in the middle of the night with my body curled around Jade's softness. At first I thought it was all part of the dream I'd had earlier. I stroked her hair, and kissed her neck. She moaned softly in her sleep.

She was fucking real.

We were both fully clothed, but it was good to just hold her. I had no idea that I could feel so much at peace by just having my woman in my arms.

Now that I'd had some sleep, I was feeling better. My eyes had adjusted to the darkness, and I could see Jade's beautiful face in the light of the moon, her long lashes sweeping across her cheeks and her lips curved into a semi-smile even as she slept.

She stirred against me, opening her eyes, she looked straight at me. We stared in wonder at one another. Yes, we needed to talk, but right now, words were not needed. Even though we both understood just how difficult our lives could become if we chose to do this, we had to decide if it was what we really wanted— and then just go for it. Together. There was no other way.

Without a doubt, I was in. One hundred percent.

CHAPTER 33

JADE

Ryder was staring at me in a way he'd never looked at me before. Usually his eyes were filled with lust, but now there was something different there. He let me look deep into his soul. Up until tonight he'd been pretty guarded, and he'd always kept his eyes hooded, to prevent anyone from seeing in. It was a protection mechanism that I'd seen Harrison use too, so I was very aware of it. It was simply their way of hiding their pain to the rest of the world.

Letting me see into his soul was a big deal for Ryder. He was so used to acting tough and ruthless all the time, never wanting to show weakness in case it was used against him, that it must have become a hard habit to break.

Maybe it was because he felt safe and loved that he was now willing to open up to me. It made me love him even more, knowing how hard it was for him to do.

"Hi," I whispered into the dark. We were the only two people here, yet it felt wrong to speak loudly. It would break the magic of the moment.

"You came back. You didn't run." Ryder's voice was filled with wonder. Reverence even.

I nodded, a big lump in my throat. He kissed my forehead, softly, gently.

"Why, Princess? Why did you come back?"

"Because . . . because even though I know our worlds are so different . . . and it will be hard on us both . . . not to mention our families . . . *I want us.*" Ryder was a straightforward man, so I gave it to him straight.

He sighed. "Yeah, I know. But it will be worth it, don't you think?"

I thought about his words before answering. It was flattering that he thought so. My heart swelled, and filled with so much love for this man that it was close to bursting.

"Yes, I guess so," I replied carefully.

"Fuck, Princess. Here I'm ready to bust my balls and do battle for you, and all you can say is 'I guess so'?"

I couldn't help myself—a small giggle escaped my lips. My Ryder was back. The man who spoke his mind, and said what he thought in no uncertain terms.

God, I loved him.

"You'll fight for me?" I asked, needing to reassure myself that I'd understood his intentions correctly.

"Fuck yeah... to the death, Princess. Because life without you ain't worth a damn."

"Really?" I breathed.

A smile twitched at the corners of his lips. "Yeah, really. I want to be with you till the last breath leaves my body."

Those words from this man's lips were so beautiful—exactly what I needed to hear.

Small circles rubbed up and down my back, making me go limp in Ryder's arms, but he had to clarify many things before I was satisfied. Especially after what he'd said before he left.

"Why the change of heart now, Ryder? What changed?"

He grinned sheepishly. "Woman, you are fucking exasperating. Cross-examining the witness till you have your answers."

"I need to know, Ryder, otherwise I'll always wonder. So if you tell me straight up, that eliminates a lot of second guessing."

"Christ. I've often thought that you'd be the best lawyer in the state. But I was wrong."

"What?" I asked, shocked at his words.

He chuckled. "Because you're gonna be the best fucking attorney in the country."

I laughed. "Pressure much? But that may just mean I'd have to prosecute your biker ass."

"Not if I'm your husband. I won't allow it."

I sucked in a breath. *What did he mean?*

"Yeah, don't look so surprised. Cause I ain't ever letting you go after tonight. Deal with it." His eyes were serious, not a trace of mockery to be seen.

"The Princess and the Badass Biker. I can just see that headline in the papers." I joked, keeping it light. I didn't want Ryder to run scared if I used the L word again—certainly not like the way he bolted the last time I'd told him I loved him.

"You gave up on us, Princess. That hurt," he said, taking me completely by surprise. Wasn't he the one who walked away? He left the city and rode his bike more than a thousand miles to get away from me. Talk about hurting.

"Why do you say that?"

"Going off with Cowboy. You were going to let him fuck you if I didn't get there in time to stop it. Fuck, I'm going to spank that ass for putting me through such agony."

My core clenched at the thought. A spanking from Ryder was erotic, and even though it hurt, he made good afterwards. I'd even risk his ire from time to time just to get a good spanking. Somehow it made the sex afterward even better, running the thin line between pain and pleasure.

"You were the one who didn't want me. You said so yourself."

"*Baby.* I've wanted you from the first moment I laid fucking eyes on you. The bossy bitch who looked down her pretty little nose at me was sexy beyond belief. You had me from day one, my Princess."

"I did? You could have fooled me."

"My cock knew even then—though my heart didn't at the time."

"Your heart?" I placed my fingertips over his heart. It was beating faster than normal. So was mine. It was beating so hard I was surprised I hadn't broken a few ribs in the process.

"My heart's a bit rusty, baby. It didn't know how much I loved you until I thought you'd moved on."

"You love me?" I whispered.

"Quit the question time. You heard me." The mischievous glint in his eyes was making my toes curl. How hard was it for him to say the three words again? I'd have to use all my lawyer skills to draw it out of him. *Ahhh, men.*

"I'm not sure what exactly I heard. I may have misunderstood. Just want to make sure we are on the same page here." I coaxed.

"As long as it's *my* page, I can live with it." He

smirked.

"Cocky, arrogant, demanding . . . hmmm . . . Let me count the ways I love thee . . ."

He laughed, a goodhearted laugh from deep within his belly. Planting a kiss on my forehead, he sighed. "Shakespeare had nothing on us. But since I'm not a dumbass biker, and you're quoting him...let me tell you something." He paused for dramatic effect, smiling at me in such a way it had my insides a-flutter. He stared directly into my eyes. "You're my fucking Juliet. I'll die for you, baby."

It wasn't exactly how I'd ever imagined having a classic quoted to me, but from Ryder's mouth it was perfect—the most romantic thing a man had ever said to me.

Just fucking perfect.

CHAPTER 34

RYDER

I'd never said those three words Jade needed to hear to a woman; and fuck me, they just wouldn't come to my lips. My heart exploded with love, with joy and happiness. Yet saying those simple three words was torture.

It was the biggest fucking deal in my whole life. Finally, I did have a name for the way I felt about Jade. Love. It was that simple, and that complex. It completely consumed me. Overwhelmed me. Brought me to my fucking knees.

There was a better way to let her know just how much I loved her. Instead of telling her, I wanted to show her. Yeah.

Cupping her face with my hand, I dipped my head and kissed her—gently, slowly, deeply—putting every ounce of my love into that one single kiss. She softened against me, kissing me back with everything she had.

Yeah, we were on the same page, alright.

It'd been so long since I'd felt her skin against mine that I was yearning to make love to her. Yeah, not just fuck her, but really make love. There was a difference; before I'd only ever fucked, but tonight I wanted to show her my love.

I kissed along her jaw, nibbling and tasting her skin till I got to her ear. I sucked a lobe into my mouth, and tugged gently. Although I was burning to get inside her, I was going to take this really slow, enjoying and worshiping everything that was Jade. She moaned softly, and I knew that the skin beneath her ear was super sensitive, so I kissed and licked that area too.

Pushing her dress down her shoulders, I growled as I took in the missing buttons on the top. Damn cowboy. How fucking dare he?

I rid her of her dress and sucked in a breath when I saw her lying there in her underwear only. God, she was so beautiful, her soft skin begging for my touch. And I would touch her—worship every inch of her skin—all night long.

Scooting off the bed, I sauntered into the bathroom. Yeah, just as I'd thought: a bath the size of a mini swimming-pool, with jets and sprays, dominated the spacious room. I ran the bath while lighting all of the fifty candles surrounding the bath. My princess deserved the best. I was going to make sure she got it.

Peering into the refrigerator, I grinned. Cowboy had stocked up on enough champagne to fill the fucking bath. Luckily we'd prefer to drink it, so I grabbed two iced flutes and the ice bucket and took it to the bathroom, filling the glasses to the brim. I slipped out of my clothing and went to get my girl.

"Hello, Big Boy." She laughed softly as she took in my cock, hard and ready for her. She lifted her hips as I pulled down her panties, and then reached back to unclip her bra, slipping it off her arms and baring her breasts to me. I stared with a salacious grin. My cock jerked in appreciation, making her laugh.

She twisted her long blond hair and knotted it on top of her head. She looked sexy as fuck with tendrils floating around her face—so feminine and beautiful it made my heart ache with love.

I lifted her off the bed and carried her to the bathroom. Her lips were dewy in the soft candlelight, inviting me to suck on them. She pressed her tits into my chest, her hard nipples grazing my skin as she did so. I set her down in the bath and followed eagerly. Sitting behind her, I pulled her to my chest as I fondled both breasts, kissing her neck. *Ahh, heaven.*

"A toast," she said as she handed me a glass. Fuck, my boys would laugh their heads off if they could see me now, in a fancy king-sized bath, candles fucking everywhere, drinking none other than girly bubbly liquid *and enjoying every fucking moment.* I was beginning to understand why Max took so much pleasure in the high life, and was trying to lure me to join him. It was addictive.

Or was it because of Jade that it was so pleasurable?

Jade turned in the bath to face me. We clinked our glasses, both smiling as we gazed into one another's eyes.

"To happiness," I said, meaning every word. She echoed my words, smiling.

Watching Jade take a sip, my heart squeezed in my chest at how adorable she was when she wrinkled her nose as the bubbles tickled her nostrils. Fuck. I'd never get enough of just *looking* at her. My cock was dying to get inside her, but it wasn't time yet.

"So," she drawled, raising a perfect eyebrow at me.

"How are we going to handle this? Because I've racked my brain, and haven't found a solution yet on how to convince Harrison that you're OK for me to be with. And Cobra; how will he take it if you hook up with me?"

I shrugged. "I honestly don't fucking know, baby. But all that matters is that we are together, yeah? I don't want to go another day without you. I'll talk to Cobra about making you my old lady."

The way her eyes widened and she nearly choked on her champagne, would've had me laughing if it wasn't such a serious matter. For more than a thousand miles on my bike, I'd thought of nothing else other than how we'd handle this. I'd mulled over every idea that came up around and around in my head. I might be able to convince Cobra; I'd known him for the best part of my life. He was my brother, for fuck's sake. Surely he wanted me to be happy, didn't he? He'd always told me how the love of a woman was the best thing any man could experience. Would he really deny me that? Even if the woman was Jade? Fuck, I'd have my work cut out, Cobra was determined to put the club first. I'd have to play on our brotherhood and hope it didn't backfire on me.

As for the angry, aggressive fucking cop? I had no fucking idea how to handle him. Yet I couldn't let him be the reason Jade and I split apart. Not now, not after all the fucking shit we'd been through. There simply had to be a way around this. I'd keep on looking for a solution, no matter how hard it was, or how long it took. Because I wanted a life with Jade. No holds barred. Without restrictions or rules.

"W . . . what?" she stammered. "Y . . . your o . . . old lady?"

"You heard me, Princess. I want your sexy ass on the back of my bike. I want to marry you. Have a shitload of babies with you." I cocked an eyebrow at her. "You have a problem with that?"

She shook her head, biting her bottom lip as she peered at me from under her lashes. I lifted her face to mine and saw that her chin was quivering, tears rimming her big blue eyes. Fuck, I wanted to make her happy, not make her cry.

"Baby," I breathed, upset that she was sad "what's wrong?" My heart was squeezing so much it felt like it would collapse in my chest. Was what I'd said so wrong that I made her cry? Fuck.

She shook her head. "No. No problem," she said, smiling through her tears. *What the fuck did that mean?* I'd never seen a woman behave like this. It was messing with my head.

"So why the tears, baby?" I rubbed my thumb over her trembling lips.

"Because you've just made me the happiest woman in the world." She blinked through the tears, her smile nearly arresting my heart.

"You're *happy*?" I was fucking gob smacked. *Women.*

"Uh-huh," she nodded, "never been happier."

I kissed the tears on her cheeks, sucking them up.

"Oh yeah?" I grinned, fucking overjoyed by her response. We were finally getting somewhere.

She refilled our glasses, and I watched as she sipped her champagne. One glass was enough for me; I'd rather have a beer or scotch. Old habits die hard. But I could see that she was enjoying it, and that was enough for me. Instead, I took hold of her foot and massaged the soles, first the one, then the other. It seemed to work like magic, because she moaned softly, and her eyes went all soft and dewy.

"Listen, I think I know how to handle this. I know

you have an apartment because Mia told me. No doubt Harrison will be on the lookout, so I won't be able to come there." I watched her face to see if she was following my train of thought. "I have access to this place in Malibu. It belongs to Max's company, and he asked me to move in years ago, but I had no need for a place then. Now I do. I'll speak to Max, and find out if his offer still stands."

"Assuming it does, what then?" she asked softly.

"If it does, I'll arrange to move in. Then you can come there in the evenings after work and over weekends." The way she bit into her lip meant she wasn't sure this would work. It was risky, but fuck, I needed to see her every day.

"Ryder, I'm not sure it's practical. What if Harrison follows me? And Cobra will be mad too because you'll put yourself at risk."

Shit. My girl was smart. Still I needed to convince her, otherwise I was fucked. "It will be tricky, I know, but we'll have to take our chances until we can work out how to handle our families. For now, it's the best solution. At least we can be together, and the place Max has ain't too shabby; you'll like it. Even has its own beach access, which makes it really private. Max installed extra security, so it's the best place for us to be together right now."

"It sounds so cloak and dagger. So dangerous. Why can't this just be simple?" She sounded exasperated. I understood exactly how she was feeling.

"Because nothing worth having ever comes cheaply. Or without fighting for. And make no mistake—I'm going to fight for this. I'm a tenacious bastard." I chuckled.

Princess had no idea what lengths I'd go to for her.

CHAPTER 35

JADE

I really wanted to believe that everything Ryder was saying was true. It would be my dream come true—to see him every day, and just be together, getting to know one another even better. But there was so much more than just the two of us involved in this.

"Do you really think that we're meant to be together? The Princess and the Biker? Or is it just a passing fantasy? Do we attract one another because we are so different, and seem exciting to one another? What if the magic wears off when the struggle becomes too hard, and you want to give up the fight? What then, Ryder?"

He sighed. "Baby, don't you understand. Now that we've come this far, there's no turning back. I know what I want. *You*. That's never going to change. Get that into your pretty little head."

I drank more champagne. I could see that Ryder

was perfectly serious. He'd thought this through, and made up his mind.

My heart knew what it wanted: Ryder. But my head was way too practical to think that this would go smoothly, without a hitch. The odds against us were practically insurmountable.

Would our love be strong enough to take us through hell just so we could be together? Only time would tell. If Ryder was willing to fight for us, then so was I. It was time to stand together as a couple, and face our challenges head on.

"I get it. Really, I do. Because I feel the same way."

The smile that split his face was reward enough. Yes. I'd made the right choice.

"I've wanted you from the first day I met you. But I'll admit that at first, it was pure lust. Your perky tits, your round ass, and your smart mouth. . . Fuck, I wanted it all." He kissed down my neck until he reached my breasts. He cupped both in his large callous hands, and sucked a nipple into his mouth. It sent a shockwave straight to my core. I pushed forward, unashamedly, wanting him to take more of me between his lips. His stubble scraped over my flesh as he moved his mouth from one breast to the other, rolling the nipple between his thumbs until I squealed in delight.

Both hands gripping my ass, he pulled me closer, so that his erection was sandwiched between us. "See what you do to me, my beautiful baby?" he asked, his pupils already dilated.

I fisted his length, stroking up and down while I squeezed his balls. His eyes rolled back in his head.

"Jesus, Princess. Be gentle. My balls want to explode."

I chuckled softly as I raised my hips from the water and sank down again, taking him inside me. I'd been dying to have him there and now I knew how much he wanted me, I also knew we would be OK. It wouldn't be easy, but hell, we had one another. That was enough for me. We'd work the rest out as we went. Now, I wanted Ryder to possess me. I wanted him to show me just how much he loved me.

He reached between us and rubbed my clit whist I rode his cock, sending the water splashing in waves around us as I rose and fell on his cock. The sensation was pure bliss, the friction driving me crazy, till I was seconds from spiraling out of control. I bit into his neck, moaning loudly as I came apart on his cock, milking him for all I was worth.

"Jesus, baby. You feel so good. My cock loves you," he croaked, swallowing hard, his Adam's apple bobbing up and down. His fingers dug into my ass as he pumped into me, calling my name.

Well, at least his cock admitted to loving me. I could live with that.

Our chests heaved as we came down from our high, knowing that this was just the start. We had the rest of our lives to look forward to—together.

Once our breathing settled, Ryder soaped my body, gently and with reverence, caressing every inch of my skin. I let him pamper me, lying back and just enjoying the pleasure of being cared for by my man.

When it was my turn, I soaped up my hands, and sitting on my heels, massaged the soap into his skin, too. He closed his eyes, humming with pleasure as I stroked his cock, cuddled his balls, and caressed his back and torso, tracing my fingers along the outline of each tattoo.

I'd noticed the new earring in his left earlobe when he'd walked into the security room hours ago, but never had the chance to comment or acknowledge it. Now I went to town; I simply couldn't resist sucking on it.

"*Baby.*" His cock hardened again. He tangled his fingers in my hair, gripping tightly.

"Suck me," he commanded, rising to sit on the raised molded chair in the corner of the triangle. Now I finally understood what those were for. He pushed his cock into my mouth, holding my head down. Cupping his balls in my hands, I took all of him, letting him fuck my mouth, listening to the panting sounds he made in appreciation.

He pulled my hair backward. His eyes were dark; he was on the edge. "Enough. Let's get back to the bedroom," he said, "got to get inside you."

I smiled up at him, happy that I could give him so much pleasure.

He stepped out of the bath and wrapped a towel around his waist. I laughed as his cock peeped out. His raging erection wasn't behaving for a second. "See how my cock can't get enough of you?" He joked as he held a towel for me.

He dried me briskly, his mouth sucking up some of the water droplets from my stomach as he dried between my legs. I moaned as his tongue rimmed my belly button. It wasn't fair; as he dried my skin, I was getting wetter.

His finger stroked between my legs as if he'd read my mind. "Wet for me, baby?" He chuckled.

"So wet, Ryder. So ready for you, baby." His eyes widened at my cheeky response. He laughed as he lifted me in his arms and carried me back to the bed. Since when did he think I was incapable of walking? I snuggled my face into his neck and breathed deeply. Yep, Ryder smelled like sex. There was just no other way to describe it. Every hormone in my body went completely wild.

He laid me on the bed, and crawled over me. "My Princess . . . my bitch," he groaned, "all mine."

He switched on the bedside lamp, and I drew in a breath when I took in the bedroom. I'd only seen it in dim light, and hadn't noticed the mirrors surrounding us, even on the ceilings. *Oh my.*

Ryder parted my legs. "Watch me as I eat you, baby," he commanded. Fuck, it was hot.

My eyes were glued to the mirror above me. I watched as his fingers spread my lips apart. We both sucked in a breath at how wet I was, my pussy glistening in the dim light. "Fuck, baby, got to taste you."

His head disappeared between my legs. God, I could have come on the very first lick over my swollen pussy. It felt so good. I moaned, unashamed, letting Ryder know just how much pleasure he was giving me. He sucked, and licked, and kissed, and slurped up my juices, all as I watched his head move over my sex. My fingers tangled in his hair, never wanting his mouth to leave my pussy. He stuck three fingers inside me, stroking against my G-spot till I couldn't handle it any longer, writhing and moaning like a slut.

"Come baby, squirt for me," he commanded.

Jesus. Fuck. I had no idea what he was talking about, but I felt a tingle so divine, from my toes to my core, hot flushes rushing over my skin, on the verge of an eruption. His fingers were relentless, driving me higher and higher till my back arched off the bed, and I screamed his name.

"Ryder! Baby!" I screamed into the night as I felt an orgasm shake my body so violently I thought I'd pass out.

"Fuck. You taste so good," he mumbled, hardly coherent himself.

"Inside. I want you inside," I whimpered as my body

rode one wave after the other.

Ryder obliged, his cock slipping in to my wetness, his breath panting in my ear.

Watching him in the mirror, his body over my body, his fingers entwined in mine, holding my arms above my head as he fucked me hard was the most beautiful thing I'd ever seen. With every thrust his ass contracted, and his thighs worked in perfect harmony as he pumped into me over and over.

"You're so fucking hot," he rumbled. "Watch me fuck you, baby." He went balls-deep, the sound of his flesh slapping against mine loudly in the silence of the night. Watching him ride me hard, my legs wrapped around his waist, my heels digging into his ass to help him go even deeper.

"Baby, I'm going to come," I cried out, stunned that I was about to follow my body into another mind-blowing orgasm.

"Come with me, Jade. I'm ready to burst." His voice was strained. He was on the very edge of no return.

I'd never known such sheer ecstasy could exist. I was lost to everything but this one perfect moment. Nothing could be better.

"Fuck. Jade, I love you!" he cried out.

I was wrong. This was better than anything.

I squeezed my eyes closed, unable to breathe as I registered his words.

"Coming baby," he growled as I lost control, and fell off the edge with him.

The force with which he pumped into me was so primal and raw. He was putting everything of himself into this very moment.

"Baby. Open your eyes, I want to see you." His voice was hardly above a whisper.

My eyes opened, and I stared into his, mere inches

from my face. What I saw made me gasp. His eyes were shining, adoration so clear it warmed the furthest corner of my soul.

"I love you, Jade. With all my heart. Only you, baby," he said, softly, a smile twitching at the corners of his mouth.

This was indeed the best moment of my life.

"Oh Ryder, I love you so much," I whispered back, scared that if I spoke too loudly, I'd break the magic spell that was woven around us. That was only the beginning of our journey together. We both wanted this. Our love was undeniable. Even though I'd fought it, never believing it could work, Ryder was showing me differently.

I wanted him and his love more than anything. I wanted to spend every hour of every day as close to him as I could be. I wanted to be his princess, his woman, his bitch . . . his old lady. I wanted to have his babies.

Sure, the future was unknown. Neither of us had a crystal ball to know how it would all turn out. We had our families to deal with, the odds were stacked against our happily ever after.

All I ever wanted was to know that I was worth fighting for. That Ryder would choose to fight for me and our love. Protect and love me. In return and would nurture and support him, loving him with all my heart.

For as long as we loved one another, we could win this battle. Our worlds collided, but we had overcome our differences so that we were now one. *Together.*

I'd be his, and he'd be mine.

Forever.

THE END

What comes after Two Worlds Colliding?

SCORPIO STINGER MC

Unchain My Heart (Book #2)

We aren't done with the story about Ryder and Jade yet.

Although they've got their happy ending (sort of), there is more to come . . .

Their worlds collided, they overcame their differences, but their journey continues. Will they stay strong and fight the forces that want to tear them apart?

Harrison Summers will make their life hell. Not only is he out to destroy MC clubs, but what happens when he finds out that Ryder is making moves on his little sister?

Cobra wants his MC brother to be happy. Just not with Jade. He doesn't want interference from a snooping cop. As president, he must make the best call for his club.

Now that Ryder has met his real father, will he also get to meet his sister? And will he, like Harrison, want to protect her against getting hurt by a damaged man?

Lexi and Razor—what happened at the club? Will Lexi get her job back at the Scorpio Stinger MC? And does she fall for Razor?

Add to GR TBR:
https://www.goodreads.com/book/show/20985987-unchain-my-heart

SCORPIO STINGER MC

Unchain My Heart (Book 2)

CHAPTER 1

RYDER

I've never been as nervous as this in my entire life. Not even when I had to go to court or was cross examined by the cops. I shook a cigarette from the packet and lit it, sucking the nicotine into my lungs. I wasn't a regular smoker, but I'd picked up the habit when I was a kid in juvie. I quickly found that it helped calm my nerves, so whenever I was about to explode with nerves, a few drags usually helped.

"Relax, Ryder. She doesn't bite." Bill laughed, but his voice was equally nervous. He was trying to reassure me, but I could tell he was apprehensive as hell himself.

"It's not every day I get to meet my half-sister for the first time. Until a few weeks ago I didn't even know she existed. And now I'm going to come face to face with her. That's a big fucking deal, Bill." He was cool with me calling him Bill, there was no way I was going to call a virtual stranger Dad just because his loins sired me.

My gaze fell on the tall brunette entering the restaurant. My mouth dropped open. She was beautiful. Elegant and perfectly poised, she could've been a model for some fancy fashion house.

She didn't smile as she walked to ward us. Her eyes were guarded beneath long black lashes and her mouth set in a determined line. I could tell she was used to getting her way. Coming to stand in front of Bill, she virtually ignored me. She didn't attempt to kiss him or anything I'd imagine a daughter would do who hadn't seen her father for a while.

"Father," she said coolly as she reached our table. Bill awkwardly tried to kiss her, but she turned her cheek and his lips barely got to touch her skin.

She looked at her watch. "Look, I don't have a lot of time. You said there was something extremely important you needed to tell me." Her gaze traveled to me and she turned her nose up slightly as she appraised me. Yeah, I was used to that from snooty bitches. Even Jade had that reaction when she first met me. A smirk curled around my lips as I sat down.

I could see she was curious as hell as to why I was here. But I'd let Bill do the talking. After all, it was his party. Both of them took their seats and stared at one another uncomfortably. I waved the waitress over. Man, I needed a beer, my throat was dry as hell.

"Anything to drink?" I asked after I ordered a large beer.

"Yes, I think I need a drink. Martini, no olives," she shot at the waitress.

Bill ordered whiskey. A triple. I could see why he needed it. "Eva, I want you to meet Ryder. That's why I asked you to come today. And because I miss you, of course." Bill's eyes were sad, his mouth turned downward. For a moment I felt sorry for the guy. To lose a wife and a daughter must've been hard on him.

For the first time, she turned to me and actually really looked at me. Her steel blue eyes were remarkable. A small smile twisted her lips as she took in my long hair tied into a ponytail and her gaze traveled up my arms and took in my tattoos.

"A new sign-up? Band or solo?" she asked.

"Neither," I grunted, taking a sip of my beer. Shit, it tasted good.

"Oh. Sorry. I thought you were a rocker. You certainly look like one."

Bill cleared his throat. "Honey, Ryder is your half-brother. I managed to trace him after all these years." His voice tapered down as she gasped, her eyes wide.

"He . . . he's my brother?" She looked at me as if I'd grown two heads.

"Yeah. Your father's indiscretion caught up with him," I drawled, amused by the surprise on her face.

"I thought you should meet. You haven't known one another as kids, but maybe . . ."

She turned to face Bill. "Why didn't you tell me over the phone that you were bringing him? You said it had something to do with Mommy. Now this?" She held up her hands, gesturing to me.

"Would you still have agreed to come? I didn't think you would." Bill said.

"Listen sweetheart, if it's okay with you, we can both walk out of here and pretend the other doesn't exist. That's fine by me. I didn't know about you till a few weeks ago. Clearly you don't need more family. I'm just fine with that, 'cause I already have a family. Nice meeting you."

Downing the rest of my beer, I pushed to my feet,

ready to leave. I didn't know what exactly to expect, but if my so-called sister didn't want to know me, there was no point in dragging this awkwardness out any longer.

She grabbed hold of my arm. "No, wait." She looked up at me from under her lashes. "I'm sorry. I behaved like a brat. It's just . . . I *hate* surprises. Daddy should know that by now. Let's have another drink and see if we can fix this bad start."

As was normal for these fancy restaurants, a waitress appeared out of nowhere. I was slowly getting used to it. We ordered another round of drinks and started chatting. At least, that's what she did. She interrogated me about my childhood, my years in juvie, and the MC club. Everything. Until I'd had enough of answering her damn questions.

"OK. That's enough about me now. Your turn. And don't skip anything." Fuck, if I could get her talking, maybe she'd quit asking me any more questions.

Bill sat back, a lot more relaxed than when we had arrived. He was on to his third triple whiskey. "Shall we order some food?" he asked, looking at the menu.

She nodded. "Why not? I'm starving. How about you, Ryder?"

Women never ceased to amaze me. Her hostility had completely melted and now she was acting as if we'd known one another our whole lives. Go figure.

"Yeah. I'll have a steak. Medium rare."

She laughed. "Oh, I doubt they do steaks here."

Bill piped up. "If Ryder wants a steak, Ryder will have a steak." He smiled at the waitress. "Please ask the chef for a special order?"

END OF EXCERPT

Please Note:
Characters from The Firebird Series: 'Lost In France'
also make an appearance in Scorpions MC ~ Ryder.

Ryder's half-brother Maxwell Grant features in Ryder's story. If you would like to read more about Max and Rebecca (Jade and Lexi's Australian cousin), you will enjoy Lost In France (Firebird Trilogy).

Although the two series are linked, it is NOT necessary to read one before the other. But if you NEED to know more about Max, he is a main character the Firebird Series.

If alpha male CEO billionaires turn you on, you will love Maxwell Grant. Add Rebecca, the feisty redhead that challenges Max all the way . . . and you have another steamy read. And did I mention Alain, the sexy Frenchman who stands in Max's way? Hmmm . . .

Firebird Trilogy

Lost in France

(Book 1 of 3)

Lost In France is an erotic contemporary romance novel set in Paris, the city of Love and Romance.

Offered a thrilling new job, Rebecca flees her tormented past, putting as much distance between herself and her ex-lover, wanting a fresh beginning in a foreign city.

On the airplane she meets Alain, a dangerously handsome Frenchman, winemaker and jetsetter, who doesn't waste time introducing her to the Mile High Club and seducing her with his French accent and charming ass-slapping ways. Sizzling chemistry with her sexy tour guide leads to a panty melting romance on the Côte d'Azur and Alain's chateau in Bordeaux. Can Rebecca find the love she is yearning for with her Frenchman?

Alain is perfect. Or so it seems.

What is his secret?

What is he hiding?

Rebecca loves her new job. It's just her alpha male boss, super arrogant CEO, Maxwell Grant, she dislikes. And Maxwell fucking Grant doesn't like her entanglement with the Frenchman.

No, he wants Rebecca to himself . . .

Is Rebecca jumping from one hotter-than-hell fire into another? And will she finally find what she is looking for?

Add to Goodreads TBR:
http://tinyurl.com/lsjw9vx

Open Your Eyes

A Standalone Novel

Is there such a thing as only one love for every person?

Is it possible to find your soul mate?

Do we deserve second chances?

Shattered and disillusioned after separating from her domineering husband, all Natalie wants, is a peaceful Christmas vacation in New York City, with her twenty-one-year-old daughter, Olivia. Uncomplicated. No pressure. Fun.

What she doesn't expect, is meeting a dangerously handsome stranger in an art gallery. He's charming, sexy as hell, and does funny things to her insides. Her frozen heart slowly melts as he seduces her, awakening her deepest desires, showing her that the kind of love she craves is very possible. She wants him as much as he wants her.

Battling his demons from the past, famous photographer Nicholas Gallagher has successfully evaded serious relationships, earning him the title of the world's most eligible bachelor. But from the moment he lays eyes on Natalie, she stirs something in him. Compelled to chase the sadness from her vivid blue eyes, Nick is captivated by the spirited Australian beauty.

Hot romance. Steamy sex. Absolute perfection.

Until Natalie gets a call from home – one she can't ignore. In a fateful moment the game changes and throws her life into chaos. Gabriel, her jealous ex, wants her back. Two powerful men want her. She is forced to make a choice that will tear her apart.

Will Natalie make the right choice? Is it possible to

love more than one person deeply? Will she finally find her soul mate, the one person who can look into her eyes and see deep into her soul, everything she is and everything she desires . . . will she finally open her eyes?

Add to your Goodreads TBR:

http://tinyurl.com/kufea2h

CONTACT DETAILS

Facebook
www.facebook.com/janikaybooks

Twitter
https://twitter.com/janikaybooks

Blog
janikaybooks.blogspot.com.au

Email
janikaybooks@gmail.com

Author Page
http://bit.ly/JaniKayAmazonPage

Jani Kay's Krusaders
Join our readers' group:
www.facebook.com/groups/256778741199366

Newsletter Link
http://tinyurl.com/msoblrd

Jani Kay would love to hear from you.
Please **email** her at:
janikaybooks@gmail.com